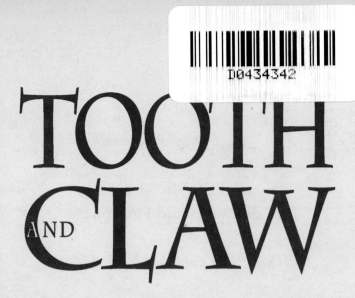

TOOTH AND CLAW

Stephen Moore lives in Newcastle upon Tyne with his wife, his young son and his cat (the cat disputes this, and claims that *they* all live with *her*).

TOOTH AND CLAW is his third novel for children. His first two, SPILLING THE MAGIC and **FIDDLESTICKS AND FIRESTONES**, are published by Hodder Children's Books.

Also by Stephen Moore:

Spilling the Magic
Fiddlesticks and Firestones

Other titles published by Hodder:

Owl Light
Maggie Pearson

Bag of Bones
Helen Cresswell

The Incredible Journey
Sheila Burnford

TOOTH AND CLAW

STEPHEN MOORE

**Hodder
Children's
Books**

a division of Hodder Headline

Typeset by Palimpsest Book Production Limited,
Polmont, Stirlingshire
Printed and bound in Great Britain by
Clays Ltd, St Ives plc

Hodder Children's Books
a division of Hodder Headline
338 Euston Road
London NW1 3BH

For Peter Moore

Contents

1. Comings and Goings   3
2. The Howling   19
3. Grundle's Ghost   26
4. A Hurt as Deep as Life   37
5. Run, or Die   44
6. The Glint of Murder   52
7. The Council of Cats   55
8. The Veil of Snow   68
9. Deep Winter Snow   77
10. The Stakeout   87
11. A Desperate Escape   97
12. At Home in the Iron Drum   114
13. Drowning   122
14. Beacon and a Tricky Knot   130
15. The Hole in the Town   138
16. Living with the Wild Cats   153
17. The Shadow Stalking   157

18. The Shadow Falling   167
19. The Field of Stones   183
20. Dart's Idea   202
21. The Gathering-in   222
22. The Great Council   229
23. Live Bait   239
24. Endings and Beginnings   257

PART ONE

Dread Booga was asleep in the dark. Hidden, like a guilty secret, beneath the town; beneath the place of men. Out of sight, out of mind. The creature spent most of its time asleep. Asleep was best. Awake it was frightened, worried, puzzled. It was certain it did not belong in this awful place, in this awful world.

Had there been an accident? Inside its injured head there were few memories. A fleeting image of breathtaking beauty; a deep black starlit sky. The certainty that at some time it had travelled a long, long way. Did it belong there, *up among the stars?*

It had not travelled alone. The delicate dried-up bones of its mate lay broken and scattered close by, where it had died. How long ago was that? A season? A lifetime? Or a hundred lifetimes?

And why did it hide? It was a creature more of spirit than of body. Its first memory of this world was the cruel, unbearable weight of a million selfish thoughts – men's thoughts – pressing in upon its own, clouding its mind, hurting it. Forcing it to escape into the darkness of the pit where men's thoughts were loth to follow. Caging it there like a wild beast, until a wild beast it had become.

There were other animals in this strange world; lesser animals than men with lesser thoughts that did not give it pain. They had seen the creature come, had run away before it.

And it was these other animals who had given it a name.

Booga, they called it.

Dread Booga.

The name tired mothers used to scare troublesome kits to sleep at night. "Shush now, or Dread Booga will come for you. Dread Booga will come."

It had become a thing of dark legend, of superstition and nightmare. Perhaps that was for the best . . .

One

COMINGS AND GOINGS

"Ow!" Mrs Ida Tupps squealed, and leapt into the air. The cat's claws dug deeper. Pierced the old woman's thick woollen jumper, her cotton blouse and winter vest. Pricked the loose warm folds of her skin beneath, and there took a tight hold.

"Ow! Ow! Ow!" With every "Ow!" Mrs Ida Tupps gave another leap into the air, hopping wildly from one ancient leg to the other. "Why, you *horrid* cat! – Miss Bryna Tupps – sticking your *nasty* little pins into me like that."

Unrepentant, Bryna's claws dug deeper still.

"Yoooo-oooOW! – I won't have you in this

3

house a minute longer. I won't. You can spend your night outside, madam. Let's see how you like that!" Mrs Ida Tupps took a deep breath, puffed herself up, and holding the young queen off at arms length, blustered her way between the sitting-room and the front door.

Bryna called out in desperation, her yowling almost as sharp a cut as her claws. And her cry said, "This is not fair. I don't care if I was sitting in your chair. I was there first! I was warm, I was tired, I was belly-full and contented. And I really, really *don't* want to be put outside!" She pushed and pulled, scratched and clawed against the arms that held her fast. But Mrs Ida Tupps did not understand. The silly old woman never understood a single word she said.

Bryna heard the front door clack open. Felt the first icy blast of midnight air. Felt herself dropped, unceremoniously, to the ground. The door was snapped shut behind

4

her with a string of muffled words. Then the pale yellow light behind the hall window was switched off.

The cold and the dark of the winter's night closed in around her. She flicked her tail stubbornly, the fur on her back twitching with annoyance. "I don't want to be outside!" she cried. "I don't want to be outside!" Nobody was listening.

Her nose was still full of old, familiar, indoor scents. The stuffy, stale air. The dry and drowsy warmth. And the peculiar, sharply sour, unnatural smell that was Mrs Ida Tupps. For a moment she remembered her food bowl, the whiteness of a saucer of milk, and the luxury of soft comfortable things to sleep on. But then, the wind began to curl around her, blowing away such thoughts, and she lost them.

Reluctantly, Bryna turned her head into the wind. All at once, the town heaped itself upon her, in a mad, confused whirl, flooding her senses; too much for the wit of a lazy, dull-brained house-cat. The brick, the stone, the iron, the glass. The crippling weight of the countless buildings, stacked remorselessly, one against the next in never-ending lines. The prickling sting of street lights. Here, the shrieking of birds in flight. There, the reek of stray cats. From far off, the soft warning smells and the tickling sounds as a river danced. And beyond, the puzzlement of dumb animals standing out upon open fields. And then in one great burst, the roar of the metal road machines – the cars and the buses, the lorries and the motorcycles – with their burning oils and choking gases. All shapes, all sizes, all mad as hell, with staring eyes that scorched the night as they charged endlessly up and down. Forever going, never getting there. And always, first and last, always and always, the heavy scents of men calling to her; this is all mine, mine, mine, mine!

Bryna's fur bristled; a new, pungent odour

stung her nose, soured her tongue, and drove away all else. At last a scent she did understand . . . dog. The stench of a dog, close by. She lifted her nose and sniffed deeply . . . A low purr rose up in her throat; this was a stale scent, yesterday's smell, and without threat.

Bryna gave herself a quick lick for confidence sake, and tried to soothe herself with thoughts of her own private outside world. Her prowl. Yes, as is the right of all cats, even this poor lap-cat has her prowl. Around and about her were the clutter of houses she took great pride in knowing by their names. There was Shipley Avenue, St Basil's, Her's Over The Road, Piggy's Lonnen and The Corner Shop. Names she had learned as a kit from Mrs Ida Tupps. Of course, *exactly* which houses matched which name she was less sure of, so she had taken to calling them all The Lonnen. It was a poor prowl then, a short walk between houses and back gardens, trees and rubbish bins, hedges and back lanes. A prowl beyond which she dared not venture. But at least it was all hers and, for the most part, trouble-free.

Satisfied at last for her safety, Bryna stalked carefully around the side of the house and headed for the back garden path.

She did not get very far. She stopped instinctively, halfway down the path. Another scent? A movement? Something odd. The undergrowth beneath the garden hedge crackled and shook. Bryna stood rigid, her eyes wide open in the darkness, body stanced, ready to run.

"Bryna? Bryna, is that you?" A tiny voice squeaked. A small, rusty-orange-and-white shape fell out of the hedge and tumbled to a standstill.

"Oh! It's only you, Treacle," Bryna said. In front of her stood a young tom, a kitten still, not a season old. She sat down heavily and turned her head away from him, pretended to ignore him.

"I'm sorry if I scared you," Treacle said, coming closer, but not quite daring to touch her. "Tupps put you out again, has she?" Without waiting for an answer, he bounded into the hedge and then out again as if he was in a chase.

"Yes, no, well . . ." Bryna licked her shoulder needlessly. "No. No, of course you didn't scare me. And of course I wasn't put out," she lied. "It was just so uncomfortably stuffy inside."

Treacle ran a quick circle around her, and deliberately fell over between her paws. "Can I come prowl with you, then?" he begged. She did not answer. Instead she turned her back on him, slipped behind the dustbin and out of the garden through a hole in the wire fence that grew up among the hedge. "Can I?" He called after her, following anyway. "I won't get in your way. Promise."

The dog was lying curled up in his own

armchair, the armchair that stood in the corner of the living-room next to the window. He was grumbling to himself. The Mister and The Missus had forgotten him, again.

The Mister and The Missus? That's what the old man and woman who lived with him called each other. And they called him Dog; when they remembered him at all, that is. His real name was Kim, he remembered that from his first home with the Kellys. Not Dog. You can't call a dog Dog, can you?

The Mister and The Missus had shut him in the living-room. They had forgotten his dinner, forgotten his walk too. And they were deaf. Stone deaf. He'd barked himself hoarse and still they hadn't heard him. Eventually, he had given up and taken to sulking in his armchair. You could see a lot from that chair. It stood in front of the window, and the curtains were never closed, day or night. Of course his eyes weren't up to much these days.

"Time for my walk," he growled sullenly. "The Kellys never forgot my walk. Not once in twelve years . . . You'll have gone to your beds, I suppose?" There was no reply.

Kim tried to listen instead, but his ears weren't any better than his eyes. Nothing seemed to work properly any more. Not at his age. His fur kept falling out in great lumps. He was out of breath at the least run. And as for his legs – oh dear, his legs would hardly keep him upright for five minutes before demanding a rest. "Long enough for a walk, though," he whined. "And there's my belly too! It's empty!" He could feel the wind building up inside him, blowing him up like a human kitten's toy balloon. He twisted himself around in his armchair and farted. "Oh, I'm much better for that. Much better for that . . ." He shut his eyes, and tried to comfort himself with sleep.

Maybe he did fall asleep, maybe he was

asleep and was only dreaming when the noises came. If only the thumping on the front door had not seemed so real; at first like fists hammering, and then like the weight of a whole body thrown against it. Suddenly, there were big bright lights swooping down through the night sky, biting holes out of the darkness. The heavy fwump, fwump, fwump of an engine. And the squeal of hard metal voices yelling commands. There were real voices too, out there in the street. Urgent voices, demanding voices. Kim lifted an ear, tried to listen, tried to understand.

"Hello? HELLO? Is there anyone in there? . . . Who lives at this one, Sarge?"

"Get that woman from next door. See if she knows owt. There's the whole ruddy street to clear!"

Thumping on the front door again, almost breaking it in.

"Violet, Violet pet, are you there?" A terrified squeak of a voice. "Violet, it's me . . .

12

Susan. SUSAN CLARKE, FROM NUMBER FORTY-FIVE." Her knuckles rapped hard against the wooden door.

"Bloody deaf old codgers." The demanding voice again. A heavy boot thudded against the door.

Kim heard movement out in the hallway. Feet clumping nervously down the stairs. Scared voices whispering. "What time's it, The Mister?"

"What you say?"

"Must be the middle of the night."

"What you say?"

"Who's there? Do you hear me, who's there?" The Missus called out weakly. "I'm warnin' you, we've got a big dog."

"What you say?"

"Violet, pet . . . IT'S MRS CLARKE. Can you come to the door?"

The click of the hall light. Door bolts clacking open. More voices in the street. Screams. Tears. Scurrying feet.

"Right. Everyone, quick as you can now. Up you come." The metal voice rang out from the sky. "No, you can't bring a great pile of luggage with you! And no, definitely no flamin' pets. We're shifting a whole ruddy town here. Not going on a ruddy holiday. Now, move along."

"What they say?"

"Eee, The Mister. I can't go climbin' up there dressed in me nightie. I'll catch me death."

"What you say?"

"And where are you takin' us, son? This is a free country. Or least, it was. Can't go draggin' respectable people out of bed in the middle of the night."

"Out of here. That's where we're taking you, missus," yelled Sarge.

"Yes, but why? This is our home, and there's all me belongin's—"

"I'll tell you why, missus – because I've been bloody well told to! That's why. Now, come on. You can put in for compensation same as everybody else!"

"What they say?"

"Look – it's an evacuation, mister. A State of Emergency. Don't you watch the telly? It was all on the news! Ruddy politicians are at each other's throats again!"

"Eee, son, you'd think two countries that's been neighbours as long as us would have run out of things to quarrel about."

"Aye, well—it's the border this time: can't even decide between them where to draw a ruddy line on the ground! So, they're giving us one each!"

"What you say?"

"A border each, coast to coast! With a ruddy great five-mile gap between them that's not going to belong to nobody. A sort of no-man's-land to stop the squabbling once and for all; and this town's right in the middle of it. You know, mister – NO-MAN'S-LAND. Like in World War One! Same as with the

bloody Germans. SAME AS WITH THE BL
– Oh, never mind! Just get moving, will you?
We've got to get out of here."

"These two the last of them?" called the
metal voice. "What? . . . No, *I said*, no animals. No exceptions."

The Machine roared louder, then louder
still, filling the whole house with its fwump,
fwump, fwump, until even the walls shook
with fear. Then it was gone, its lights disappearing over the rooftops.

Kim suddenly realised – he hadn't barked
once. Not a whimper. Hadn't even jumped
down from his chair to scratch at the door.
Well, you don't, do you, not when it's a
dream? And it was a dream, *wasn't it*? He
shuffled himself about and, far too warm and
comfortable to worry any more about it, lost
himself inside a deeper sleep.

"Do you think it's safe, Bryna? Do you think
it's safe to go home yet?" Treacle whispered

from the hiding place he'd found for himself deep inside the privet hedge.

"I'm, I'm not sure." Bryna was hiding close by, in the same hedge, her eyes screwed up tight shut. They'd been hiding most of the night. Ever since those awful machines had flown at them out of the night sky. Bryna knew about the metal birds – the aeroplanes. She expected to find them way up in the sky, safely out of reach and harm's way. But these machines weren't the same at all. They flew very, very low, stood still upon the air, had huge arching lights that chased you across the ground, growling voices that made terrible threatening noises. And the noises had been contagious. There had been banging on front doors, people spilling out on to the streets, noisy with fear and panic. Then the grumble of the traffic out on the main roads had become suddenly too loud, as if there was far too much of it. In fact, the whole town had become suddenly too loud.

That was when Bryna and Treacle had taken to the hedge, and they were still hiding there, long after the town had gone quiet again.

"I'll, I'll go and have a look," Bryna said, pretending to be brave. She opened her eyes slowly and carefully – just in case she saw something she did not want to see – and cautiously poked her head out from behind the leaf cover. It was getting light. The bitter cold and the stark blackness of the night was relenting, and a cloudy sky was being stroked by a cheerless early-morning sun. The hairs on her nose twitched. The air around her was almost still, almost motionless. No one, nothing, was about.

At last, she stepped out into the open and, as her bravery grew with the light of day, she began her prowl home.

"Bryna, are you still there? Can I come out now?" Treacle cried, still too scared to move. But for Bryna, the kit was already long forgotten.

Two

THE HOWLING

Bryna sat down upon Mrs Ida Tupps' back doorstep, her ears twitching as she listened for the sounds of familiar morning movements. That unexplainable nonsense beloved of all men. The ritual coughs, the sneezes, the chinking and the clanking, the banging about. The wooden sounds of creaking floorboards as clumsy human feet stomped sleepily from room to room. Clicking things, twisting things. Picking things up, putting things down again.

But not this morning. No, not this morning. The house stood silent. There were no sounds, no movements. And it never once occurred to Bryna, after all the strange adventures of the night, that there would not be.

"I'm hungry! Let me in, *I'm hungry*—!" She mewed, certain still that Mrs Ida Tupps would answer her cries. Soon the door would be opened up with soft words, with delicious, back-tingling strokes, and a fuss. All Bryna had to do was wait. Just wait.

But it was a very long wait, with no more story to it than the passage of time.

Mrs Ida Tupps did not come and open up the door.

Later, the sun lifted its pale head above the roof line only to disappear behind a curtain of soft grey cloud. Rain spat upon the ground in tiny feathered droplets, thought better of it and dried up again.

Mrs Ida Tupps did not come and open up the door.

At length, it was a sudden plaintive mewing that finally distracted Bryna. She stood up, turned open-eyed and spat her irritation at the approaching intruder; only to find Treacle coming towards her down the garden path.

"Oh Bryna, Bryna, where have all the people gone?" the kit mewed pitifully. "Nobody will answer my calls. There isn't a man anywhere! Not anywhere! And I think I'm starving to death." He was shaking uncontrollably, and his paws left damp patches on the pavement behind him.

Bryna flicked her tail, thoughtfully, felt the pain of hunger tighten in her belly. She looked from the house to the kit, and back again, unsure of what to make of it. The windows and doors were shut, the curtains were still closed. That was wrong. She paced around to the front of the house, with Treacle following anxiously, unwilling to let her out of his sight. Out on the pavement the street lamps were still burning in the broad daylight. Surely that was wrong too? And there was something else. Or rather, there wasn't something else when there should have been.

"Listen, Treacle. Listen," she said. Where was the constant roaring? The never-ending shriek of car engines? The screams of gears and brakes as they chased each other about the streets in their usual mindless hurry? It was deathly quiet. Even the roads were wrong. Bryna licked her shoulder, confused, annoyed. How had she not noticed until now?

"I'm scared," Treacle whimpered, huddling himself up into a tiny ball. "Something horrible has happened, I just know it."

"Let's see." Bryna drew her ears flat against her head, opened her throat and gave a long-practised, sorrowful caterwaul. That cry always opened a window somewhere. Treacle was so impressed he stopped shaking for a moment, and stood up expectantly.

But the houses did not reply. The Lonnen stayed stubbornly silent.

And then, without any warning, it started . . . *the howling*.

It was far away at first. Beyond The Lonnen and the allotments, behind the swanky new houses. Past the waterside factories, way out across the river.

Bryna's ears pricked at the sound. Across her back her fur rucked nervously.

"What's that? What is it?" Treacle cried.

"It sounds like a dog . . . a dog calling." Bryna's head began to ache. This was no ordinary noise. What dog could possibly make a sound like that? Not a whine, or a yowl, it was more sorrowful, more pitiful than both. The call of an animal lost, hopelessly lost. Suddenly, from somewhere down upon the riverside, a second dog joined in. And closer still a third; and then another, and another . . . The town began to fill up with hopeless screams. Dogs, dogs everywhere, were howling. And surely not only dogs, but cats too; cats screaming their heads off.

Treacle's eyes blinked saucer-wide with fear, he stanced low, and with fur bristling backed against the larger she-cat.

Bryna could not move. Mesmerised by the unreal cries, she had to listen, desperate for them to explain themselves.

And then the spell broke. A dog was barking in The Lonnen. His voice heavy and morose, but real. Definitely real. "That's Kim," spat Treacle. "The Mister's old black mongrel, at number forty-seven. He must still be locked up in the sitting-room. And the best place for him!"

"Of course. Of course!" Bryna said. Her ears pricked. The howling did tell her something. "The crying dogs, the screaming cats, they're all like Kim! All trapped, locked up, shut inside their houses. And there's nobody to let them out."

"You mean, just like there's nobody to let us in?" Treacle whimpered.

"Yes," Bryna said, and she licked frantically

at her paws, as the full weight of the awful truth began to settle on her shoulders . . . The whole of mankind had gone from the town. And yet, how could that be? How could that possibly be? Men were like the sun, the wind and the rain. Like the day and the night. Like the stones of the ground and the birds of the air. Like the endless hate between dog and cat. Part of life. Always, always there. And if they were not there, then – then what?

Black clouds thickened across the grey sky. Rain came again, and properly this time. Hard, cold rain, that cut the fur from the body. The dogs still howled. When the rain came a third time Mrs Ida Tupps' front doorstep was in darkness. The dogs had fallen silent. The cats were gone.

Three

GRUNDLE'S GHOST

Sodden to the skin, Bryna moved silently down the garden path and out into the street. Behind her, the young kit followed.

Where were they going, these foolish house-cats? Force of habit kept Bryna to the familiar trail of her prowl, but in truth they did not know where they were going. Their world had changed forever that day, and they were moving away from the house, stirred by some ancient instinct they could not name. That, and the cruel gnawing of their empty bellies.

They stopped more than once at over-turned rubbish bins and picked at scraps. But it always seemed that some other cat had been there before them and the sting of hunger was only worsened by the lingering smells. For them food had always appeared on demand, been rattled from cardboard boxes, spilled from glass bottles, or scraped from tin cans with soft kittish words. They had been forever pampered and fed like helpless blind kits. Indeed, everything in their lives, everything they were, had come from man. Even their names were only sentimental parodies of men's own – or else some clever trick played with human words for their own amusement – they did not truly belong to them.

And what of wild nature? What of the chase, the hunt, and the sweetness of the kill? Just silly games of play, and Catch-me-if-you-can. And if a little later they found themselves trying to stalk a sparrow? It was nothing planned.

They'd come to a place where a deep thicket of bushes nestled up against a high garden wall. A foolish bird fluttered across the wall and dropped to the ground just out of their paws' reach. Instinctively Bryna stiffened, stanced very low as if she was trying to hide herself beneath the cover of dead leaves that lay there.

"Food at last!" Treacle hissed, clumsily copying her actions.

"Shhhh! Quiet . . . You'll scare it away."

But the odd little bird didn't seem to notice them there, intent as it was upon feeding itself.

For a long moment Bryna didn't move. Inside her dull house-cat's head there were vague, woolly thoughts. She remembered the lick of a warm sun upon her back as it streamed through an upstairs window. Remembered stretching deliciously, idly looking down upon a large grey tom cat, as he crouched among the bushes in the garden below. Dexter, was that his name? Yes, Dexter. Somewhere nearby was his mate –

a heavy white queen called Fat Blossom –
but she was even more vague and did not
concern Bryna. What mattered, what she
remembered most was the tom hunting.
Hunting for birds.

Bryna sniffed the air. There were no recent
cat scents, no Dexters or Fat Blossoms. The
sparrow was still feeding happily. There was
a chance yet.

Unfortunately, Bryna did not understand
the first thing about catching birds. Oh
yes, she'd often watched the grey tom but
she'd never really given it much thought.
Until now, hunting had seemed such a silly,
undignified and messy way of going about
finding food. For one thing, birds never
stood still long enough to catch. For another,
they were as fragile as the wind that carries
them across the sky. And when you did
finally get your claws into one of them,
what was the reward? A mouthful of fluff
and broken feather! It had been so much

simpler to play begging-kitten with Mrs Ida Tupps. Easy meat, every time.

"Aren't we supposed to do it *now*?" whispered Treacle, a purr of excitement thrumming in his throat. "Bryna—?" The sparrow had hopped a step closer, was almost asking to be caught.

Bryna tried desperately to remember how Dexter had gone about his hunt. She was already crouched flat, that felt right. She began to strum the ground with her back legs, tensing and flexing her muscles in readiness. "Jump, Treacle," she cried. "Jump!"

They jumped together.

Bryna's claws extended, her body stretched, curled up like a spring, and burst open again, sending her flying through the air. Her whiskers felt the feathered air whisked up by the beat of the sparrow's frantic wings. The bird was within her grasp.

"Where's it gone?" hissed Treacle, baffled. "I had it, had it right there in my claws—!"

"So did I!" cried Bryna.

The rat-tat-tat of agitated bird calls filled the empty space where the sparrow should have been. Treacle's eyes blazed with frustration, he leapt through the bushes and ran off across the garden, desperate to catch it up.

"Don't be daft, Treacle, it's too late," mewed Bryna, half-turning to see where he was going. "You'll never ca—" And there she stopped, frozen to the spot, and forgot all about Treacle.

In front of her stood the biggest, the ugliest, and the dirtiest tom cat she had ever seen. He was a smudgy, charcoal-ginger in colour, with a head as big and broad and heavy as the whole of Bryna put together. And the way he stanced gave Bryna the strange idea that somehow he wasn't quite real. His body looked stuffed, like a human kit's battered old cuddly toy. His eyes were like odd shirt buttons with colours that didn't match, and his stuffing was leaking out through his mouth.

"This what you're after pussy-cat – a nice fat sparrow?" he hissed through clenched teeth, and dropped the carcass of the bird he'd been carrying. Bryna hissed back, and tried desperately to blow herself up to his size. The tom just laughed, pushed his nose into her face, and said, very, very softly, "Boo."

Bryna fell over her own paws, went scuttling backwards, until she felt the weight of the garden wall behind her. She had not meant to run. It was just that, well . . . she did not know what it was. She picked herself up, used the wall to steady herself. "Who – who are you?" she squeaked at him. She had meant her cry to sound angry, but it came out thin and weak. "And it's been raining all night so why aren't you wet?" Her cry stopped coming out altogether after that. It was such a stupid thing to say, even if it was true. She was drenched and the rain was still falling hard enough to sting her eyes. So, why was this cat dry? Bone dry? Why had she not heard his approach, or caught his scent on the air? And worse, why couldn't she smell him even now?

It was easily explained ... Bryna had just met her first ghost. Yes, ghost. Not such a strange thing among those of her kind. (And in time there will be other ghosts to put greater twists into the flick of her tail.)

Almost without knowing it, in a kind of involuntary slow motion, her legs began to pull her backwards, away from him, following the length of the wall.

"I think the pussy-cat's leaving us, Grundle," the ghost said, as if he was talking to another cat over his shoulder. There was no another cat. He was talking to himself. "Kitty-witty frit of a tired old stray, eh, Grundle?" Another look over his shoulder. His voice was mocking her, the way that all wild cats – even dead ones – mocked all house-cats. At least that was something normal about him.

Bryna was still walking backwards in slow motion. She never once took her eyes off his. At last she could see why they looked so odd: one eye was a deep sea-green in colour and sparkled with mischief; but the other, the other was a dull pinky-grey and thick with scars. Grundle was completely blind in that eye. Or at least he should have been. The way that eye stared at her it seemed to see a lot more than his good eye ever could.

Bryna tried to say something, but her voice was still lost somewhere in her throat; and more strangely still, inside her head a shadow began to fall; as if the weight of the ghost grew heavy upon her.

Suddenly Grundle was very close. So close, if he'd been breathing she would have felt the tickle of his breath on her nose. "Not hungry any more then, kitty?" he said. "Pretty little collar too tight for you to swallow?" He laughed at his own joke, his throat throbbing with a raw, self-satisfied purr. He lifted a paw and pushed the remains of his dead bird towards her. "Go on, take it. Take it! It won't bite you."

Bryna did not – could not – move.

Suddenly, the dead bird squawked and leapt into the air, cack-cackering at the petrified cat. Then, still screaming, it turned and landed neatly on Grundle's shoulder.

At last Bryna found her voice; even if she did not recognise the noise she made. She found her legs too, sprang straight upwards, and in one gigantic leap landed on top of the garden wall. Grundle only laughed louder, and the bird on his shoulder laughed with him. "Did we scare the poor little pussy-wussy then?"

Bryna jumped down behind the wall, found herself running hard down a cinder path that led her between two houses. The whole world had gone mad and her aching head was full up with pictures of Grundle's huge, one-eyed, laughing face.

Bryna ran on blindly; out of the claws of one problem . . . into the jaws of another . . .

Four

A HURT AS DEEP AS LIFE

The dog, Kim, had at last decided that his dream had not been a dream after all. No, he was just going mad, like some old dogs do. He had been stuck on his own, in that living-room, all night and all day. And now it was the middle of the night again, and he was still there. He hadn't heard a single noise from The Mister or The Missus. Not one. Of course, the awful silence was probably just part of his madness.

"I'm still here," he whined. "I'm still here. And a dog can't hold his bladder for ever. Not at my age."

Not a peep. Not from the house, not from the streets outside. Earlier he had heard a cat calling, and dogs had started to howl. He had even joined in, done his share. But it was just crying. No animal was making any sense. So he had stopped, and eventually the others had stopped too. Now there was just the sound of the rain, and when you get used to that it's just as good as dead quiet.

He thought about his stomach, and the burning thirst in his mouth. He was getting too old for this kind of silly lark.

And then Kim found himself pacing around the room (again), jumping up into his arm-chair (again), looking out of the window on to the empty street (again). He'd been doing an awful lot of that and he wasn't expecting this time to be any different to the last. Out of the window it would be dark, except where the ever-burning lamplight caught against the falling rain and the wet outline of the tree that stood in the garden. There would be nothing of interest outside.

But there was.

There was a cat! A cat as large as life and bold as brass, charging across *his* front garden. Cheeky ruddy animal! That was when he found out he really was going mad. Or why else did he suddenly launch himself from his armchair, straight at the window, like a daft, over-excited puppy? There was an odd echoing fwump as his dead weight bounced back off the glass.

The cat should have scooted then, instinctively panicked. But it didn't. Instead, it did the opposite: it stood still: as if it understood something about the glass barrier that kept them safely apart. When Kim climbed back into the armchair to take another look, there it was, standing in the middle of the garden, staring right back at him in a funny, uncomfortable way. What was the matter with the stupid thing? Was it mad too?

"Don't you know a ruddy dog when you see one?" he roared at it, and deliberately hurled himself at the window again. There was another sickening fwump as he hit the glass. Panting, winded, he steadied himself before slowly clawing his way back into his chair. The stupid cat was still there! "Rowf! Rowf—!"

The third time he hit the window the sound was different; like the air was being broken up into tiny little shreds, like it was being murdered. And he could feel its sudden pain, like he was being broken up too.

His madness was complete. Up until that moment there had only ever been one world. Only one, Kim was certain of that. But not now, now there were definitely two: an outside world, and an inside world. And they were both calling to him.

He found himself lying stretched out on the ground. It was raining, bitterly cold, and he was wet, and the wetness and the cold soothed him. That was the outside world. But there was another world, on the inside, and all he knew there was a terrible hurt. A terrible, terrible hurt.

He thought he remembered a window breaking, and a hideous scream that surely must have been his own. The window and the scream were part of the inside world, part of the terrible hurt. And he knew he must get out of that inside world, or else . . . or else stay there, forever.

He opened his eyes the best he could.

There was a tree in front of him. And around him wet grass. In among the grass the rain was turning into tiny puddles, a million of them, and all sparkling. Not soft and round and wet puddles, but hard puddles, jagged-edged, glittering and angry. Spilling across his legs and body.

There was broken glass everywhere.

He wanted to move away from it, but knew that if he did the hurt would reclaim him, take him back into the inside world forever.

He lifted his eyes to the tree. There was

41

that cat again! It was a snotty-nosed young tortoiseshell. Name of Bryna. Lived up the street some ways off. She was clinging to the branches at the top of the tree as if her life depended on it. Well, maybe it did.

"What you ruddy well doing up my ruddy tree, cat?" He thought he growled at her. But if he did, it didn't have the desired effect. Bryna began making her way gingerly down the trunk of the small tree – backside first. Then she crossed the grass between them, came right up to him, did not stop, not even when he growled again.

Kim knew there was a wound in his belly. An open gash. The sweet scent of blood lay heavily upon the air smothering everything else. And his blood mixed with the rain and ran in rivers through his matted fur. It was a hurt as deep as life itself. But he was still alive, still breathing.

"Come to gloat, cat . . ." Kim's mouth did not seem to want to move with his words.

"Come to laugh at my last breath?" He hoped his eyes still glared with contempt, even now, half-closed, heavy with the pain. "Never could stand cats . . ."

At last he gave in, his two worlds collided, merged together, and left only the empty darkness.

Five

RUN, OR DIE

Why didn't Bryna run away from Kim when she first saw him behind the window? Why did she stand over him now, watching as he fell into unconsciousness? He was a dog, wasn't he? And she was a cat? And dogs and cats hated each other, didn't they? That was how it was. That was the rule. You could rely on it. And yet, nothing seemed to make sense any more. Maybe that was even part of the answer. Houses without people; sore, empty bellies; and an aching head that came and went at the strangest of times, had come worst of all with Grundle's ghost. At least an injured animal, even a dying dog, was something real, something she could understand.

Bryna began to lick the deep wound in Kim's belly, cleaning it of dirt. She carefully used her claws to scrape away the ugly shards of glass. Then, she gently lay down, rested her body up against his, used her small weight as a pressure to help seal his wound, to halt the flow of life from his body. She felt his blood seeping slowly into her fur.

And there Bryna stayed, and at last slept, overtaken by weariness, even after the rain had stopped, and the first hint of morning light broke the darkness.

She would have stayed there longer . . . if she had not been attacked.

"Grrrrr, Rawf! Rawf!"

"Kill the bloody murderess. Rawf!"

Dogs, there were dogs everywhere. Dogs tumbling towards her from all directions. Dogs, unpractised at killing, stumbling in their eagerness. A wild mix of breeds, all sizes, all strengths, their angry teeth bared. Bryna tried to cry out as she came fully awake, but her scream was wasted, drowned out by their furious roar. "Murderess! Rawf! Rawf! Rawf!"

Now she must run, or die. No time to think. No time to protest innocence. *Run, or die.* Almost together, a huge German Shepherd and a small, scruffy-looking Yorkshire Terrier were the first to land their blows. *Run, or die.*

Bryna's open claws raked the muzzle of the bigger dog as she pulled herself free of Kim's limp body, felt the dry blood that bound them together tear apart. She twisted, and scrambled her way up and over the backs of the dog pack. The cat who flew, the dogs called her, and perhaps she did fly. Jaws snapped shut, teeth bit hard. Fur and skin tore beneath her as she struggled free. In her panic, if it was her own, she felt no sting. And then, at last, her legs touched solid ground again, and her paws found a grip that was enough to run with.

And she did run. On and on, never stopping, not even to see where it was she went. Not until the yowls of the dogs, and the frantic scraping of their claws against the pavement as they gave chase, were nothing more than a memory on the new morning's wind.

Beneath some bush somewhere, she stood still a moment to find her breath, before running on aimlessly. At some roadside puddle, heavy with engine oil, she took a drink. Among fallen leaves and windborne papers gathered against some old stone wall she fell, exhausted. Beyond fear, or care. And there she slept again. The fretful nightmarish sleep of the hunted.

When she woke up, she was sick with hunger. Her eyes would not open, and she could not lift her head. It stayed stubbornly on the ground, too heavy, thick and fuddled to be moved. The hunger pain in her belly was matched by a second pain in her shoulder where the terrier's teeth had bitten deeply. Already the wound was a poisoned sore. She battled with her head again, and eventually managed to pull it up off the ground. She licked and bit blindly at her wound until it bled cleanly.

Slowly, she became used to the empty sickness in her belly, and her head cleared enough for her to find her balance, and stand up. But when she finally opened her eyes the sight that confronted her almost knocked her down again. She was standing on high ground, and could see just how far her blind run from the dogs had brought her. There, spread out below her, was her whole world: the great grey body of the town, caught asleep beneath a cold winter sun. There was no colour to it: the shining yellow streetlamps had finally gone out. It was as if the town had somehow lost its last great struggle for life and now lay dead. An empty shell, a carcass waiting to be picked over by scavengers. And at its very heart ran a dull grey river, snaking lazily, cutting the dead town in half; with only a bridge defiantly holding the two sides together.

Bryna began to move downhill, some weak instinct demanding that she retraced her steps. It was a long, long walk, and the pain in her wounded shoulder bit deep with every stride. Later, she remembered nothing of the way she took, of the streets or the roads. The sounds and pictures of the previous two days would not stop filling her head. It came as a total surprise when she found herself limping along The Lonnen.

There was not a dog or a cat to be seen anywhere. Where Kim had lain in front of the broken window there was a crusted pool of blood, like a frozen crimson lake. But there was no body. No scattered remains either. He was not dead then. Walked away or carried away? How? The puzzle was too great for her, and now her muddled head was filling up with food again, or rather, with a woozy sickness for the lack of it.

Somewhere a small brown bird called out to her. "Isn't this what you're looking for?" she thought it said.

And then there was another voice. A real voice. "Bryna, where have you been? Bryna, are you hurt. What's the matter with you? Oh, just look what I've got – See, it's a bird, a bird to eat. Dexter's been teaching us how to catch them properly. Dexter says all the people really have deserted us, just like we thought. They've gone from everywhere and there's not one left. Not one, not in the whole town. Bryna? Dexter says the dogs have packed together, and we've got to watch out for them. Dexter says they're killers. And oh – Dexter says there's to be a Council and we've all got to be there. Bryna, Dexter says—"

"Treacle, don't you ever stop for breath?"

"Oh, but Bryna, every cat's going. I-I can't stop, I've got to find Lodger, got to tell him the news. Dexter says meet at the allotments. Tonight. Oh, and you can have this—"

Treacle pawed his dead sparrow towards her, and bounded off down the street.

Bryna swallowed the small bird head first, and in one go, was promptly sick, and ate it again more carefully. The second time it stayed down.

Six

THE GLINT OF MURDER

Was he dead? Kim wondered. He felt very sore, very weak and painfully thirsty. He didn't *feel* dead. Then again, he didn't really know what dead felt like.

When he had opened his eyes, there had been dogs standing silently over him. Watching him? Guarding him? They were still there, only now there seemed to be an argument going on. Or, or was some dog making a speech?

"You see, you see," a German Shepherd roared, "see what the cats have done to this poor dog. Look at his wound, brothers! If we had not attacked when we did that murdering queen would have killed him for sure." As if to make his point, he pawed the fresh wound on his own muzzle, making it bleed.

"Aye, Khan, you're right there! Bloody cats! They're all murderers, thieving murderers at that," yapped a Yorkshire Terrier in agreement. "Just wait and see, brothers. They'll be stealing the food right out of our puppies' mouths next." The other dogs began to grumble uneasily.

Kim lifted his head, wanted to tell them all not to be *so* stupid, but a heavy paw pushed it back to the ground. Khan ranted on. "It's up to us dogs – now that our masters are called away – it's our duty to protect the town against their scourge. What do you say, Yip-yap?"

"Aye, aye, rid the town of the cats! Rid the town of the cats!" the Yorkshire Terrier chorused, nipping dogs close by him until they joined in with his chant.

"Rid the town of the cats!" The cry went up, and the air filled with hysterical yowls and barks. Kim tried to move again, but found himself still pinned to the ground by the massive paws of a Great Dane. "Daft beggars," he whined. "That cat saved my life. She *saved* my life." No dog was listening. "Oh well, please yourselves, stupid fools . . ." The hurt of his wound began pulling at him again, and he felt himself falling back into the safety of unconsciousness.

He did not see the dogs gathering wildly for the hunt. He did not see them start off, Khan and Yip-yap leading the way, the glint of murder shining in their eyes.

Seven

THE COUNCIL OF CATS

The night came bitterly cold, and the darkening sky was further blackened with big heavy clouds that would surely bring snow. Bryna was not the first to arrive at the allotments. There were several cats already gathered there. The strong mix of fresh odours, and the slight movements of the night air against her whiskers told her that much. To one side of her, beyond a patch of carefully turned grey earth, she sensed a young queen sitting among a stretch of tall weeds and grasses. She was brindle-marked and had been named Brindle after her colouring (a common practice among lazy men). Directly in front of Brindle, at the end of a short cinder path, a home-made greenhouse – a chaos of old house doors and windows frames – was being guarded by a pair of large black toms. Bryna limped slowly along the cinder path and sat down to wait beneath a rusting wheelbarrow that stood to the side of the greenhouse. She made no sound, and stared blankly out into the night, careful to ignore the other cats. Who they were she would know soon enough; it was not polite to ask questions, even of a stranger, before a Council.

Soon there were nearer fifteen or twenty cats on the allotments; all sitting discreetly apart, politely ignoring their neighbours. Among them was Treacle, as anxious and agitated as ever. He was sitting under the broken wooden boundary fence, strumming his claws through a discarded plastic carrier bag for comfort. There too was Lodger, skulking behind an empty, overturned dustbin.

The old tabby had always liked to pretend he lived alone and independent; wild as the feral cats rumoured to prowl the Town Moor on the opposite banks of the river. In reality he'd spent the best part of his days asleep on the rug next to the oven, in the back kitchen of a house in Cedar Drive. It had been a house full of ever-changing students who had always kept up the rule of leaving a window open for him so that he could come and go as he pleased. Well, not any more. And Lodger was no longer pretending.

Dexter arrived silently, and on his own. He walked slowly and leisurely through the mixed assortment of cats waiting there. The large black toms guarding the greenhouse watched him intently, moved silently aside as he approached. They were his bodyguard. With a careless ease, and without breaking his step, Dexter jumped up onto the wheelbarrow and up again onto the roof of the greenhouse. There, he sat down and did some waiting of his own. He was a very beautiful cat, large, but fine-boned with short grey hair. His eyes were bright and inquisitive, and stared expectantly, back along the way he had come. Eventually, plodding along in his footsteps there followed a second cat. She wheezed and puffed heavily with every step, and in between she hissed and spat, moaned and grumbled, enough to wake the dead.

"Oh Dexter, Dexter, wait for me, will you? Wait for me. Urgh! This ground's too wet. Look at my poor fur – we won't be staying out here *all* night, will we? And what's this sticking to my paws—?" This was Fat Blossom. Dexter's companion. At last she reached the wheelbarrow. She stanced down low, as if she was about to jump, but only her eyes followed Dexter to the roof of the greenhouse. Instead of jumping up, she sat down heavily, and clumsily; as if even that was far more than enough exercise for one evening.

Somewhere, out among the ranks of gathered cats, kits began to snigger. Fat Blossom's

eyes shone with fury. It was always told after-
wards how that look of hers cut through the
dark and landed a blow on the heads of
the young revellers as heavy as any tom's
closed paw. Whatever the truth, the ranks
fell silent. Bryna's head began to ache
as she watched, ached in that strange,
indescribable way that she knew now as
a sign of ... well, as a sign of something not quite normal. There was, perhaps, more to this strange Fat Blossom
than met the eye.

Unnoticed, Dexter had stood up. He
opened his throat and called out the formal
greeting, "Welcome stranger*." At once,
from all around the allotment, the gentle

---

* Welcome stranger, though not always used, is the
formal and proper address between one cat and
another, whether the cats know each other or not. Cats
never, *ever*, use the plural! It is every cat's conceit that
it is the most important animal in the whole world, and
to be thus generalised would be beyond sufferance.

throb of contented purring lifted into the night air.

"Welcome stranger," cats began to answer him in turn. "Welcome stranger."

But already there were cats who were worried beyond politeness.

"Never mind the welcome stranger," some cat called out. "I want to know what the heck's goin' on?" Instantly, the purring stopped. All eyes turned upon Dexter. And then every cat was yelling out at the same time.

"Yes, tell us that, if you can? What's going on, Dexter . . . ?"

"Where's our food?"

"And where have all the people gone to?"

"And what are you going to do about the dogs?"

"'Aye, aye, dogs is everywhere."

"Bloody killers too! I seen 'em at it. Only a kitten it was."

The black toms guarding the greenhouse raised themselves to their full height, and stanced for attack. Fat Blossom began pacing backwards and forwards in front of Bryna's wheelbarrow, angrily grumbling and muttering to herself.

Then a thin, shrill voice cried out, "Look what they've done to *my* leg. Look! Nearly torn off it is." There was more worried commotion, tails flicked and cats began to mew, as a small tiger-marked kit hobbled forwards, dragging his useless hind leg along the ground behind him. As he moved, a tiny bell fixed to his collar tinkled, and seemed to call out his name . . . Maxwell . . . Maxwell . . .

Bryna heard Fat Blossom's sharp intake of breath; it was almost as if she knew what was to follow. Within three paces of the greenhouse the injured kit stumbled and fell. Maxwell lay there, stricken, his breathing heavy and laboured, unable to move further.

All around cats were standing up, agitated tails stretched up into the air. The heavy scent of fear burned Bryna's nostrils.

"Well, Dexter, just look at that," mewed a large brown tabby, who seemed to have cats gathering at his side. "You called the Council! So what are you goin' to do about it?"

Dexter threw back his head and caterwauled for silence.

"My friends, listen to me. Hear me out! . . . We must stay calm. We must look at the facts." He looked down at Fat Blossom for support. She turned upon the squabbling cats, tried to stare them into silence. But not even her worst look could shut them up this time.

"The facts are we'll soon be starving to death!" came a sharp reply.

"Yes! We're not filthy strays. Can't go eatin' any old rubbish."

"And we're not *all* uncivilised hunters!" cried the tabby.

"We are all hungry," Dexter hissed. "But we must face the truth, and we must do it together. Mankind has abandoned us. They have gone from the town, and left us to our fate. Their houses are closed against us. Their windows are locked, their doors are bolted."

"And maybe we're the lucky ones!" For the first time, Brindle, who was still sitting in among the weeds, spoke out. "We, at least, are locked on the outside of their houses, where there's hope. There are plenty of cats who are not so lucky. My own mate is a prisoner behind a locked door. What chance does he have?"

"Aye, I've heard them," mewed Lodger, from behind his rubbish bin. "The pitiful crying of trapped cats. The yowling of dogs."

"Never mind the mangy dogs!" squealed the tabby. "Aren't there enough of them roamin' free for us to worry about? Chargin' about in packs, killin' and murderin' innocent animals!"

Bryna flicked her ears this way and that,

listening to the arguments rage on all sides of her. Cats, she decided, weren't really much good in large groups.

"Please, please. One cat at a time," Dexter called. "And listen . . . We must organise. We must decide what is to be done – and we must do it together."

"Well, I, for one, have had enough of all this twaddle," spat Brindle. "I'll look after myself, if it's all the same to you." She stood up and began to stalk off through the grass.

"Yes—" Dexter cried after her. "I'm sure you can look after yourself, queen. You are young and strong, with all your wits about you. You'll manage all right. You'll feed your own belly. Let the others fend for themselves. The old, the injured, and the kits—"

"Pah!" spat Brindle, without looking back.

"And you are no doubt big enough and strong enough to take on an entire dog pack on your own."

Brindle stood still, but without turning.

Other voices began their cat calls again.

"Together," continued Dexter, "only together, can we survive until man's return."

"Yes, yes, Dexter is right," cried some cat. "We must hunt together for food. Give each other protection. Guard against the dogs." Bryna twitched her ears in the direction of the voice. This made sense.

"No! This is foolish talk," cried the tabby. "What happens if the people never come back? Eh, what happens then? . . . No, we can't wait here. We must go after them. Seek them out for ourselves."

"Aye, aye . . ." mewed young toms and excited kits desperate for adventure.

"And it's each for themselves, as is the cats' way," said Brindle.

Bryna's ears twitched again. This too made sense.

Close by, Fat Blossom had stopped her grumbling, and now stood alert, her eyes nervously searching the dark. Bryna felt a sharp coldness as a shadow fell across her mind, sensed Fat Blossom's strange change of mood. Dexter too sensed her mood and began to climb down from the greenhouse roof. He knew things were not going well. He knew there was no agreement near making, and now, he knew there was something else . . . something far worse.

"What is it, Blossom?" he asked.

"Dexter, it's the dogs!" Fat Blossom cried out. "THE DOGS!"

Out of the night the dogs fell upon the cats.

Bryna's body froze, locked in panic, in fear, refused to move. Only her mind raced frantically. Why had they gathered together so openly? Brindle had been right. They should have listened to her. Bryna had already survived the dog pack on her own. It could be done. She could learn the sly ways of the stray, of the wild cat. She could live out on the streets, on her own, or, or maybe take

Treacle with her. Yes, yes, she could take Treacle with her. But this, *this* . . .

Out of the night the dogs fell upon the cats.

In their Council the cats had grown careless, forgetful of everything but their own squabbles and arguments. Not a single nose had sniffed the dog scent. Not one ear had heard the clumsy thumping of dog paws, the heavy panting of their breath. Even Fat Blossom had allowed herself to become absorbed in their futile debate . . . until the last moment, until it was too late.

And what of this Dexter, this would-be leader of cats? Hadn't he placed watchers? A guard of his own choosing? Hadn't he, surely?

Where they had stood at street corners, now they lay dead.

Out of the night the dogs fell upon the cats.

"Grrrowf, growf, rowf—"

Eight

THE VEIL OF SNOW

Which came first, the snow, the ghost, or the crying of injured animals? No cat can know for sure. Let us say for the sake of our story, and to save us from the bloody gore of a death fight, that it was the snow . . . It tumbled out of the cold night sky, blinding white, dropped like a dazzling curtain, instantly blotting out everything.

Bryna stood there watching the snow, still paralysed, helpless with fear.

Then, a voice spoke to her in urgent whispers. "Quickly now, pussy-wussy. Come this way. There are no dogs to fear this way!" Surely it was not a real voice, not a voice blown about on the wind or muffled behind the weight of falling snow. And yet, it was a voice she knew.

"Who, who's there?" she called to it.

"No time to play guessy-games, moggy. Escape is this way!"

For a moment Bryna was sure she saw Grundle through the veil of snow; dead Grundle, standing there, with his small bird perched upon his back. And then at last, she did move, as she began to hear the fierce roars and caterwauls of fighting cats and dogs; the yowls of the stricken and the struggle for life itself. She stumbled blindly forwards, hoping to find the spot where the ghost of Grundle had stood. But the snowstorm beat itself against her in violent flurries, like some big bully, forcing her to move the wrong way.

She tried to turn against it, tried to make her way to where she could hear the thick of the fighting. But whichever way she moved, she never seemed to get anywhere before the sounds moved off to some other place.

The snow fell heavier still, until even the yelling and screaming were lost within its thickening blanket. Soon there was only its endless empty whiteness, that and the stinging bite of its chill.

It was a cat's paw that found her at last.

"Here's another one—"

"Alive?"

Bryna could not find her voice to answer the question herself.

"Aye, alive. But she's frozen to the bone."

Then, two anxious black faces, both heavily marked from fierce fighting and glistening with the spillage of fresh blood, loomed at her out of the snow.

"Come on, we've got to get you out of this storm!"

Bryna followed their flicking black tails through the falling snow without a thought for where they were taking her. Almost at once, they were climbing: first uphill, she could feel the ground rising beneath her paws, and then just up. Where before snow had been striking her face, the strokes of loose twigs were hitting her now, as if they were in among the bare branches of a tree. When the black tails in front of her suddenly disappeared Bryna panicked and leapt forward. The bare branches, the snow and the chill of the night were all instantly gone.

It was suddenly very quiet, and very peaceful, like the weatherless peaceful inside of Mrs Ida Tupps' living-room, full of dusty human smells and stale human air. The black cats had brought her to a room, a small and untidy room, full of the litter of a human kitten. They *had* climbed a tree and from it jumped through an open bedroom window.

Fat Blossom was sitting on the windowsill, mumbling numbers to herself, counting off cats as they fell in through the window. At least Bryna supposed it was Fat Blossom: even in the dark she could see that her great white body had turned a kind of vivid pink. Bryna sensed other cats too, already sitting silently about the room. But how many were there she couldn't tell. The stench of fear clung so heavily to the air it masked all but the strongest of cat scents. She did recognise Brindle, hidden deep within the shadows of the room, and the kitten Treacle. Yes, she was sure Treacle was there too, somewhere.

As Fat Blossom's count reached fifteen, the weight of Bryna's old shoulder wound, the hunger, the cold and the fear, stole the last of her strength and she began to drift into a fitful sleep.

Some time later, she was half-awakened by cats mewing anxiously at her side. Fat Blossom's voice came to her first, as vague murmurings; coaxing, pacifying . . . and then more clearly Dexter's voice, bitter and anguished, "I should have been more careful," he spat. "I should have known where it would end."

"How could you have known?" said Fat Blossom.

"I . . . I should have guessed. It was obvious. Bringing the cats together, all in one place. How could I have been so stupid!"

"But there had to be a Council—"

"Did there? Did there really? And what did it achieve? They would have been better off on their own. Fending for themselves."

"We brought some cats to safety, at least."

"Oh yes, battered and broken for the most part. And what of the rest? Those we left behind, those we left for dead, what have we done for them? Tell me that. What have we done for them?"

Bryna couldn't lie still any longer and lifted her head towards the voices. Instantly, the argument stopped without an answer. "Dexter, is that you?" she asked drowsily, trying to look for him in the dark. Beautiful Dexter. The cat in front of her was his size, his shape. But the face, surely the face was all wrong? What had the dogs done with Dexter's beautiful face? She closed her eyes again. Slunk down into the bed clothes. Shut him out. Forced herself to sleep.

PART TWO

Dread Booga stirred in its sleep. Not enough to wake up, only enough to stretch out its long thin arms and delight in the feeling of strength returning to its fragile, naked body. Something outside, something out there in the town had changed. Its injured head was not so fuddled now, not so heavy with the weight of men's thoughts, and that was a blessed relief.

There were other things too, things it had not known in a very long time . . . The desire to move about in the open, unfettered. The pangs of hunger gnawing at its belly.

Its clawed fingers were tingling with a peculiar eagerness, and it knew, even if it did not, could not *understand, that there was a kind of power, a strange force within those fingers desperate to be unleashed . . .*

PART TWO

Nine

DEEP WINTER SNOW

The sun danced across the walls of the bedroom; a sprinkling of light tossed backwards and forwards as the branches of the tree outside the window were rocked by a slight gust of wind. Slowly the sunlight came to rest again, landing on the bed where Bryna lay, and she gave herself up to its delicious warmth. It was so good to be waking up at home again. Oh, it was so, so good—

But then around her she began to sense other cats; their scents, their slight movements, the noise of their breathing. And with the cats she remembered. Remembered everything. This was not her home. She lay very still, wanted the warmth of the sun to send her back to sleep. But it would not.

She struggled stiffly to her feet.

Lying next to her, not a tail's length away, was a thin, poor-looking brown tabby, lost in a restless sleep. Next to the tabby lay the kit, Maxwell; his collar and bell were missing, and his injured leg was twisted awkwardly underneath his body as if it did not really belong to him. How had any cat managed to save him? And if his rescue was not impossible enough, lying at the head of the bed raised up on a pillow was a young mother with three blind newborns frantically suckling at her swollen teats. Fat Blossom was sitting on the floor close by, and Dexter was on the windowsill, with his back turned against her.

"You're awake at last, Bryna," Fat Blossom said, jumping clumsily onto the bed, forcing the cheery purr she had needed with most of the injured cats. "Your shoulder wound – I see it's healing well."

"Oh, this old thing. It's nothing." Bryna returned the purr as best she could. Her shoulder throbbed with pain, and the heavy scab had broken open and was weeping. They were both telling lies, and somehow they both knew.

They eyed each other quizzically. For Bryna it was as if she was seeing something of herself in that fat white cat; the part of her that saw ghosts, and had peculiar, unexplainable feelings. Then the moment was past.

"I think you're ready for your breakfast." This time Fat Blossom's soft purr was real. As she spoke a small orange-and-white kit heaved himself in through the open window, and without a glance at Dexter, fell clumsily onto the bed, dropping the warm body of a mouse between Bryna's paws.

"Welcome stranger," said Treacle, laughing.

And so the winter days turned slowly over.

It was the hardest of times: the snows came worse and worse again, settling deeper and more treacherous with each new fall. The brown tabby who had slept at Bryna's side died after three days. Silently, the pair of black toms – Dexter's bodyguard – removed his body between them. There were others too, who had rested upon the floor beneath the bed. Bryna did not see them alive and she did not see them dead. Fat Blossom's daily head count fell to twelve.

For those cats who survived, that small bedroom became their home after all. Home, refuge, hospital, and ultimately prison. There was a door that led from the room to the rest of the house, but it was firmly closed and no amount of clawing made any difference. The only way to get out was to jump through the open window and climb down the trunk of the tree into the front garden. And once outside the streets were always dangerous. The snow was nothing less than a death trap, its deepest drifts making movement impossible for all but the biggest of the cats. And anywhere the wind happened to blow a pavement clear of snow there were always dogs, dogs sitting in wait of them.

And what of filling their empty bellies? There was little for the hunters among them to stalk; the snow and the dogs saw to that. What could be scavenged from the streets was done by lone cats late at night, or more daringly, during the heaviest falls of snow when the dogs did not venture outside. Any scrap that could be carried was brought back to the bedroom to be shared out equally among them all. At first that meant rich pickings – if a cat knew where to look – whole chicken carcasses, fat-rich bacon rinds, half-eaten tins of meat. What could not be carried – the slops scraped from dinner plates, the broken raw eggs, dribbles of congealed cooking fat, and other such treasures – well, finders keepers.

But soon, all too soon, rubbish bins and street droppings were picked clean. Dogs had been there first, or other cats, and more than once, some unnamed wild animal who left behind a scent that worried the nose and sent the heart beating strangely. And once bins were emptied they stayed emptied: there were no more wasteful humans endlessly filling them up again.

"Dexter, we must have more food," Fat Blossom said, looking anxiously at the three tiny blind bundles nuzzling uselessly at their exhausted mother. "Crumpet is so very weak now. I don't think her kits will last another night . . ."

Dexter stood silently looking out of the window, watching the snow fall. He did not answer. He did not have an answer.

That night Fat Blossom's count of twelve cats became ten . . . only the largest of the newborns clung on to life.

In the days that followed scavenging cats

began to return home empty-handed, often desperate and angry, and cursing the gangs of dogs who had chased them to within an inch of their lives. Others brought reports of lone dogs seen lurking quietly in shadowed doorways: dogs carefully placed at regular intervals, street by street, like frontline troops, and effectively cutting off whole districts of the town to all but the slyest of cats. Sometimes, just sometimes, other cats were seen. Dexter called all of these reports *Intelligence*, and he praised cats for it, although Bryna was never really sure why. "It's the next best thing there is to food," he would say and rub a paw against his empty belly. Bryna would have settled for the food.

With more and more Intelligence, and less and less food, with each new day, the condition of the cats grew steadily worse. Skin began to hang loose from ribs, and fur became dull and patchy. Dexter was unaccountably thinner and more patchy than the rest. Even Fat Blossom stopped looking quite so fat.

And if this was not enough, cats injured in the dog-fight at the allotments simply never got fully better. Wounds would not heal properly; they leaked continually, or became poisoned, or bled afresh through each newly formed scab. Of course, no cat complained. How could they ever complain, with Dexter? He made nothing of his battle wounds, but Bryna was never quite able to look him in the face. Even now there was a gash across his skull that lay open to the bone. His left ear had been chewed to a bloodied tat, and a cruel double line, gouged by dog fangs, ran down his nose and under his jaw. It left his mouth with a permanent sneering grin, that forever dribbled blood, or food, or saliva.

With his Intelligence Dexter tried to build up a picture of animal movements on their side of the river. It became clear from sightings that they were not the only cats to survive. There was a small group, perhaps half a mile away, probably based around a street called Waverley Crescent. And another that prowled the derelict, Year of Enterprise, Youth Employment Project warehouses that skirted the river just below the bridge. It was also clear that there were a few loners – old Lodger among them – still roaming free outside.

Of what had become of the dogs Dexter was even more certain. They were highly organised and patrolled the streets like an army of occupation. Lone sentries stood guard on street corners, while small packs of two or three dogs endlessly hunted for unwary cats. From reports of their numbers and movements the main pack seemed to be centred around the area of the town Bryna called The Lonnen, though no cat ever dared to venture close enough to prove it.

On the other hand, that the dogs knew for certain of their whereabouts was obvious, with or without Intelligence. More than once already, a dog patrol had trailed a scavenging cat back to their tree, only to be thwarted as he or she scampered out of jaws' reach. And sometimes, while Bryna sat at the window, she would see a dog lurking at the top of the street, quietly watching them. These sightings, seldom at first, became more frequent as the first chill of winter relented, and the snows began to clear.

Ten

THE STAKEOUT

And then one morning, the dogs became bolder still.

"Bryna, come and look at this," said Treacle.

"Oh, what is it? Can't you let me sleep?" Bryna was dozing happily on the bed. "There are blessed few other pleasures left to me!" She turned over and stretched sullenly, not wanting to be bothered.

Treacle had an irritating habit of calling cats to the window to see the silliest of kittish things. Yesterday it had been a windblown plastic carrier bag that had come floating across the street, snagging itself on a branch in their tree. And then there were his dog games; he was always seeing dogs in the shadows of garden hedges, dogs creeping along the street, or slinking into doorways. Dogs who were never there.

"Bryna, quickly – *Please.* You must come to the window," Treacle insisted, his pleas getting more urgent with every word. "The dogs. Look at the dogs."

"Dogs?" Bryna sniffed at the air sceptically. But her ears stiffened automatically. "Oh, all right, seeing as I won't get a moment's peace until I do."

Reluctantly, she sat up, and jumped onto the windowsill at Treacle's side. Her sudden movement was met by a deep threatening growl from under their tree. There was Khan himself; pack leader, and a giant of a German Shepherd. He was sitting happily in their garden, his head cocked mockingly to one side, and his tongue lolling carelessly from his mouth. He could have been begging for a game of chase and fetch. Next to him stood a much smaller dog, the iron-jawed terrier, Yip-yap. Bryna remembered them both very well. It was Yip-yap who was growling.

"Coming out to play, kitty-kitty?" he barked.

The skin on Bryna's back tingled as her hair rose, her ears dropped flat and with her eyes exploding with fury she hissed and spat.

Then Treacle joined in, copying Bryna's movements like a shadow. "I'll show the cocky so-and-so's." He would have leapt straight out of the window if Bryna had not clawed him back by the scruff of his neck.

"Not quite so fast," Bryna hissed. "That's just what they want us to do."

"Just let me get one of them on their own. That's all, just let me—"

The window suddenly rattled in its frame and the kit tumbled off the windowsill and scuttled beneath the bed. His voice had been drowned out by a new noise, dreadful and foreboding in its intensity, filling the room.

Bryna tried to close her ears to it, tried not to run scared, dug her claws into the wood of the windowsill, and held herself there.

Khan was barking.

Of the ten cats who made up the lodge, five were out on prowl: Dexter, Fat Blossom, the pair of black toms, and the solitary queen, Brindle. That left Bryna, Treacle, Crumpet with her tiny kit, and the injured Maxwell. Not much of a stand to put up against Khan! At least the dogs were down in the street, and they were up in the bedroom, so they were safe enough. Or at least, they should have been; with the German Shepherd so close, it was somehow impossible to feel completely safe.

Bryna kept up her defiant stance at the window. Somehow she felt responsible for the lodge now. When the dogs barked their taunts at her she taunted them back with loud caterwauls of her own. "You're not scaring me, *little* doggies. Got no rubber bones to play with?" And even as Khan and Yip-yap laughed at her, it made her feel stronger.

At midday the sun stood high above the tree, reflecting a blinding white light off the melting snow. The dogs were still there. And worse, now there were four of them, and no sign of any returning cat. A little later Khan and Yip-yap marched off down the street with as much showing off, pomp and ceremony as they could muster. Almost at once their vacant spot under the tree was taken by a new pair of dogs. From then on, there was a regular changing of the guard. And as each pair of dogs came and went they would always make a noisy show of it. Dancing and yapping in mock battle, or barking and growling up at the window. The dogs were there to stay, and they wanted the cats to know it . . .

"Sssssst! Sssssst! . . . 'ryna."

Bryna was still sitting at the window – she hadn't moved since the dogs had appeared

– and at first heard nothing but the wind fiddling with the branches of the tree. Beneath her she could clearly see four guard dogs, tails and paws stretched out, nestling up against one another. Asleep in the snow.

"Ssssst . . . sssst . . ."

Bryna's ears pricked.

"Ssssst . . . sssst . . . are oo deaf dow' air?" said the strange voice.

"*Dexter*? Is that you, Dexter?" Puzzled, Bryna stood up and looked about her. There was nothing to see. Below her the dogs were still sleeping peacefully. But there was a strange sense of some cat or some *thing* watching over her—

"Uf ear. Ook uf ear!" the voice insisted.

Cautiously, Bryna pushed her head through the open window. She twisted it almost to the point of snapping it off, until she was looking up and not down. Suddenly, she came face to face with a big, boggle-eyed, floppy-mouthed fish.

"Qui'ly 'ryna! Tay i', qui'ly, pleath!" it said. And then, at last, Bryna began to understand. Dexter was hanging by his back paws from the metal guttering that ran beneath the roof of the house. The fish was dangling out of his mouth. "Qui'ly! 'Efore I dro'i'. 'Efore I 'all. Uh 'ish. Tay 'old o' uh 'ish." Bryna grabbed the fish and tugged, and together – fish and cat – fell backwards into the room. Outside there was a raking and snapping of branches and twigs, and Dexter scrambled in through the window after her. From below came the sleepy yowling of dogs and a frustrated thwump thwump thwump as, one after another, they began throwing themselves at the trunk of the tree.

"There's nothing like fresh fish. That's what I always say," Dexter laughed.

"But where did you find it?" Bryna didn't quite believe her eyes, or the taste on her tongue. Dexter didn't answer, just pawed the fish playfully towards her. Treacle appeared sheepishly from beneath the bed, and then all around them cats who a minute before had decided their end was upon them, suddenly changed their minds and decided it was meal-time instead. Each cat took their share. Every cat but Dexter, that is. Bryna tried to be like him. Tried to say no when she looked at the way the meagre shares were gulped down greedily, disappearing without a trace into the bellies of the starving cats: only enough food to remind them of their deep hunger. She tried to say no, but she could not.

Dexter sat down and watched them eat, and as he did he began to purr. It was a gentle, strangely sad purr, like a tom's last goodbye to his favourite queen.

Only when the meal was finished did any cat remember the cats who were missing. "Where are the others?" Maxwell asked innocently, from his place on the sickbed.

"They are waiting," said Dexter, simply. "They are waiting for us."

"Waiting for us?" repeated Treacle, as if the words didn't make any sense.

Dexter nodded. "It's time for us to leave. It's no longer safe to stay here. You must see that?" As if on cue, out on the street, the dogs began to bark again. And their noise, their smell, their heavy lumbering thoughts seemed to creep upwards, filling the room, turning the sweet taste of fish in their throats to a sour bile.

Bryna's eyes grew wide and she began to pace about the room, staring up at the walls as if they would suddenly open up and give her a new way out.

Crumpet staggered weakly to her feet, holding her last newborn protectively to herself. "Just listen to them out there. Just listen to them! Crying for the blood of my kit . . ."

Dexter hung his head sadly, lifted a paw

and cuffed a ball of dust that had gathered on the bedroom carpet. For a brief moment, he was just a silly kitten again, just a silly kitten playing. If only, oh, if only . . .

Eleven

A DESPERATE ESCAPE

Already it was the middle of the night. Dexter was sitting up on the window ledge, listening . . . Below him, at the foot of the tree, the guard dogs were silent. By the near stillness of the night air and the shallow rhythmic sounds of breathing, he was sure there were only three dogs now, and that they had at last fallen asleep. He had been waiting patiently for this moment. There wouldn't be a better chance for the cats to make their escape.

"It's time. Don't make a sound, and please, try to keep up with me," he said. And that was all he said. Then he moved, stood up and jumped from the window to the branches of the tree in one action.

Bryna looked hopelessly at the poor rag-tag of cats who stood up in their turn, each desperate to find the courage to follow Dexter out into the night. But none did. Maxwell's back leg was so badly hurt he could hardly stand. Crumpet – the young mother – nervously held her tiny kit close to her, watching helplessly as it cried silently for the comfort of her teat. And Treacle was no more than a big kit himself, grown too gaunt and gangly for the lack of proper food. How could these cats possibly make a run for it through a pack of dogs?

"If I've got to climb up on to the roof I won't make it," Maxwell said quietly, matter-of-factly. "I won't, I'm not strong enough. Might as well leave me behind. And you can't expect that tiny kit to go chasing through the night."

"Listen," Bryna said, "we must trust Dexter. He's brought us this far, hasn't he? Kept us alive? Well, now he's asking us to follow him again, so we must follow him. And if he says run, then we must run. Run until our hearts burst." Treacle mewed in agreement.

"I've run far enough," said Crumpet, sitting down heavily.

"We'll see," said Bryna. She scooped up the crying kit from its mother's side, took it firmly in her mouth, and started after Dexter.

With a squeal of pure anguish Crumpet chased after her; instinctively refusing to let her last surviving kit out of her sight. Treacle followed Bryna's lead, and shouldered Maxwell forward, bullied him towards the window.

Outside, Dexter had climbed quickly to the top of the tree, and was looking intently along the darkened street. Bryna felt the branch beneath her paws bend as it took first her weight, and then the weight of the others behind her. Crumpet was still protesting furiously, and worse, was disturbing the snow, sending it fluttering to the ground. There was no room to turn around, but somehow Bryna managed to lift the tiny kit over her shoulder, and she pushed it into the eager, open mouth of its mother.

"There! Now please, *shut up*," she hissed. It was already too late. Beneath them, a dog growled softly in his sleep, stirred and scratched himself, cocked an ear to the night.

Dexter was not about to lose any more cats, but before he could move, before he could climb down through the branches of the tree and push them all back through the open window, there came the loud, defiant crying of a cat some way off up the street. The crying of a cat ready to do battle, that broke the silence of the night for good. It was Fat Blossom, calling the dogs to her with curses and dirt. Daring them to chase her, daring them to fight. Almost in the same instant, Brindle's voice joined in from a second direction. And then came the deep sombre caterwauls of the black toms from a third and a fourth.

If the guard dogs had been asleep they weren't now. They were all standing at the bottom of the tree, tails erect, ears held high. Heavy rolling growls playing in their throats. But they held back, refusing to be coaxed away from their guard.

"Listen to that lot, the cheeky beggars. We ought to give them what for."

"We must stay here. Khan's instructions. And anyway, they'll have to come this way sooner or later. If they ever want to climb back into their lodge."

"Aye, aye, that's all well and good, but just listen to them."

Fat Blossom cried out again. "Not scared of a few wee pussy cats, are you?" The dogs' growls grew louder, rattling with spittle through their teeth. But still they would not be tempted away from the tree. Bryna sensed Fat Blossom's movement before she saw her;

her white fur glowing like a full moon under the cloudless evening sky. She was standing in the middle of the road, hardly more than a shadow's length away from the tree, and now within easy striking distance. If the dogs decided to attack she could easily be caught.

"Bow wow little doggies!" she cried, and then she laughed, laughed as hard as she could.

"Right, right, that does it. I'm not listening to any more of this, you little—" The dogs charged at her heedless, pounced together at the spot where she had been standing. Pounced, only to find her gone, only to find her suddenly replaced by four cats, where before she had been alone. The dogs lashed out in all directions, their teeth snapping shut, tearing off lumps of thin air, or at best their own tongues.

"Grrrr, growf! Growf! What the blazes—?"

Cats there. Cats gone. Cats there, cats gone

again. Just like phantoms, just like ghosts. Exactly like ghosts. And if the dogs did not understand, Bryna did. Just for a moment, right there in the thick of the fight, she recognised a brown tabby cat; the very cat who had shared her bed in the lodge, until he'd been carried out dead.

And then Fat Blossom was on her own again, bounding off up the street, to where the black toms and Brindle lay waiting, ready to make their attack as the dogs gave chase.

Dexter did not stand still while the dogs fought Fat Blossom's ghosts. He brought the cats down out of the tree and headed them in the opposite direction. Led them a good prowl's length without stopping. He kept to sidestreets, back lanes and lonnens, short cuts beneath hedgerows, and across snow-patched waste grounds. His route curled and twisted, and more than once retraced the tracks they had already taken, in an effort to confuse would-be pursuers. Bryna was soon lost, but Dexter strode on confidently. There were at least two other cat lodges in the town and he knew where to find them. (All his gathering of Intelligence had told him that.)

At the next street corner, to Bryna's surprise, Brindle was waiting for them on her own. Dexter did not stop, or even look her way, and silently she tagged along behind the last cat in line. Before long one of the pair of black toms was there too; Bryna had never known them to be separated.

"Not far now," Dexter called gently, coaxing them onward, giving no sign that he was worried over Fat Blossom's absence. When the wind began to turn against them, he called again. "Not far, my kittens. Keep up . . ." But the night air was suddenly too fresh. Where the wind blew it was too empty of signs. There were no proper smells or tastes, no clear sounds.

It began to snow heavily, and the wind

whipped it up and hurled it at them in blinding flurries, so that it stung their eyes and cut into their fur, freezing there.

"Not far now . . ." Dexter called out, a third time. Bryna kept moving, concentrated on following the tail in front of her. Trusted her life to that tail. Although their way seemed suddenly less sure now, less certain, paws were faltering . . .

And then, walking with her, stride for stride, there was another cat. A cat who left no mark in the snow behind him. A huge charcoal-ginger tom with a strange little bird sitting on his back.

Grundle. Her own dead Grundle.

Bryna's head ached again, and a dull grey heaviness filled her up inside. "What is it?" she asked, but already the ghost was gone. He'd said nothing, had given no words of warning, but Bryna suddenly knew—

"Dexter, the dogs—" she wailed, and saw, through the falling snow, Khan leaping from a wall. "Dexter!" She heard the dog's great front paws thud upon the ground, heard his roar, and felt the surge of air as he pounced to the attack, as the dog pack followed his lead. And she saw, saw from that other part of her self she could not name, that she would never see Dexter alive again. Not Dexter, not Fat Blossom, not Maxwell nor Brindle . . .

There was confusion then, and panic. In the thickening snowfall they had let themselves be caught upon a narrow path between two high walls. It wasn't a planned ambush. The dog pack had simply stumbled across them in their blind search. Bryna bounded forwards, leapt for the top of the stone wall only to fall back again. Then she turned and ran. Just ran. What or who she ran from, what or who came running after her, she did not know.

"Wait, Bryna. Please, wait. It's me – it's Treacle. We can't keep up—" For an instant Bryna looked back across her shoulder, but without letting up. There at her tail ran Treacle and Crumpet (with her kit still held firmly in her mouth). Behind them a storm of snow blurred the night air, made shadows of the death fight.

"Can't stop," Bryna yelled. "Can't. Can't."

More walls jumped over, street corners skittered around, dustbins turned over as they catapulted themselves from obstacle to obstacle, forcing themselves on. And then, the smell of fear, the crying of cats, the heavy panting of dogs in pursuit, was gone.

"M-must stop—" Treacle gasped, stumbled, and fell so heavily against Bryna and the young mother he nearly brought them all to the ground. "Bryna, please?"

"For a moment, then," Bryna said. "But only for a moment, or they'll be on to us again." She lifted her head and looked about her anxiously, trying to make out where it was they had stopped. They were in the middle of a large open space. It was not a garden; there was something hard – concrete or tarmac – under the snow, and a long way off there were walls closing them in. Behind them, a pair of large wooden gates with a man's name hand-painted on one side flapped open and shut, as they were rattled by the wind. The cats had run through the gates, run themselves to safety.

Bryna began to relax, to take long breaths, trying to rid her head of the insanity of the chase. Treacle was still gasping, but he was not really hurt. It was Crumpet who was the worry: her eyes fretted, her breath kicked fitfully and would not settle, and her whole body shook with fear. In her mouth her kit hung limply. It was dead. It would be fruitless to carry the poor thing any further, and yet, and yet . . .

Suddenly, there came the noise of running again; the muffled scrat-pat scrat-pat of paws working hard against snow and pavement. Some dog had caught on to their scent and was turning in through the gates as they swung open. The cats tried to move, but their legs would not go, as shock and renewed fear held them where they stood. The dog's snarl bubbled up through its throat, its sickly breath filled the night air as it barked its hatred, its contempt. And then, just as suddenly as it had appeared, it stopped its charge, and fell silent.

A heavy wet nose came to within an inch of Bryna's, and sniffed. "Grrrr . . . well well, what do we have here? . . . I suppose, I suppose I should bite your bloody heads off." And then the dog laughed. "But these old wounds of mine are slowing me down. And I'm not as young as I was. You were a bit too quick for me."

Bryna didn't understand.

"Aye, too nimble! You must have got yourselves over that wall there, run off down by the river, maybe got yourselves across that bridge before I could catch you up."

Still Bryna didn't understand. And yet, even through her fear she sensed something familiar about this dog. Its smell, its taste, the way its breath came, the way it moved. If only her eyes weren't stricken – blinded with terror – she would know him for certain.

Out on the street other dogs began to bark, and paws came running. "Kim – that you in there? What you got yourself then, what you found?"

"Of course—" said Bryna.

"Shut it! And say nowt, cat," said Kim. "Say nowt, and stay alive." The old black mongrel turned towards the gates. "That's us evens," he whispered. "Your life for my life, and I'll throw in your friends here for free." Then he barked loudly in answer to his companions. "There's nowt much in here. Trail's gone cold. Must've been rats or something."

A pair of nosey snouts pushed eagerly through the gates only to be pushed back out again. "Don't waste your time here, try the other side of the road. Looks like some animal's been disturbing the fresh snow . . ." Kim's voice trailed off as he led the dogs away from the cats' hiding place.

Treacle stared blankly between Bryna and the petrified Crumpet. He did not understand why they were still alive.

Bryna opened her mouth to explain, but it was not her voice that spoke then. Being still alive wasn't the last surprise of that strange night.

"Right then, you lot, you'd better come along with me. Can't stay out here in the open. Some cats are just not safe to be let out on their own. Some cats ought to know better, getting themselves mixed up with dogs." A big, baggy old tom cat had appeared out of nowhere, and was standing close behind them.

"Lodger, is that really you?"

Lodger didn't answer. Instead, he gently took the dead kit from Crumpet's mouth and quietly laid it out of sight beneath the shadows of the far wall. When he returned and ushered them forwards with a gentle push, when he climbed a pile of broken brickwork to reach the top of the wall, the three cats mindlessly followed.

"Bah, house-cats," he muttered, "all the same they are. Want to be kittens all their lives. Want a mother to nursemaid them. People to wash them, people to feed them, fussing about with their coochy-coos . . ."

He led them at last to the riverside, to an overturned iron drum he called his lodge. In the dark it could have been anywhere. And if Bryna thought anything, she thought how much the old rusted drum, and the baggy old tom cat were alike. Both were aged, both weather-worn, and both – strangest of all – were the same muddy ginger colour. Where the rust had eaten a hole in one end of the drum Lodger had made an entrance. Inside, the sharp, sour smell of the rust hurt their noses until they grew accustomed to it; but at least it was dry, and safe, and with the shreds of newspapers and bits of rag that littered the floor, it was warm enough.

Here, at last, they gave themselves up to sleep.

Twelve

AT HOME IN THE IRON DRUM

For two days and two nights neither Bryna, Treacle nor Crumpet stirred from their beds inside the iron drum. Lodger busied himself with his comings and goings, content for now to leave them to sleep off their misery. He always returned home with his mouth full, bringing them mice or voles or birds, and once, even a scrape of lard clinging to a piece of paper.

When the three cats were not asleep they sat, or lay about in a brooding, uneasy silence. For Bryna there was nothing left to say. The world had become such a horrible, horrible place.

On the third day Lodger had had enough,

and he pushed them all out into the snow. "Can't go moping about after the dead for ever. Life goes on, you know," he snapped at them, nipping their heels, driving them out through the hole in the drum. "So get yourselves out there and fetch in your own dinner. I want my home to myself for a change." He marched himself back into the drum, sat down, and pushed his backside out of the hole, blocking it up. Bryna was so startled by such rough treatment from the old cat she simply picked herself up and went to do as she'd been told: to find her own dinner.

"Wait, Bryna! Wait for us," Treacle and Crumpet cried after her. "We're coming with you . . ."

And so, once more, the short days and the long nights of winter passed by, one upon the next. The streets were never clear of snow. Snowstorms came and went, and then came again heaviest just when the cats thought they had seen the last of it. "Longest, cruelest winter I've ever seen," Lodger said.

But there was, at least, one joy for Bryna; their lodge, the iron drum. It sat almost on the edge of the riverbank, and was well protected from prying eyes by a kind of big hill that grew up behind it. Lodger said the hill was what men called a rubbish tip, and it was piled high with the strangest things. There were bits of everything and everything was in bits. Broken chairs, threadbare pieces of carpet, beds, china, plastic bags – thousands of plastic bags – clothes, plastic washing-up bowls, dead plants, hedge cuttings, marmalade jars, tin cans, rotting potatoes and more: and all dumped at the edge of the river. Bryna would never understand people.

Sometimes, just sometimes, the winter sun would shine, and the cats would raid the hill for a convenient scrap of cardboard or piece of carpet maybe, and laze happily at the water's edge. When they wanted solitude, to think, or simply to be alone, there were endless nooks and crannies, holes and shallow caves to be explored. Temporary homes were even found there, when silly arguments sent huffy cats storming out of the drum. They served too as hidey-holes into which they could easily escape when inquisitive bands of dogs ventured too close to the riverside for comfort. (The rubbish tip's pungent, stale odours masked their own, and the dogs would pass by none the wiser.)

There was never a safe time to hunt; cats would steal out on to the riverside streets only when their bellies got the better of them. And Lodger made them promise to prowl alone. "Alone is best," he said, "only yourself to look after. Only yourself to get caught by dogs." And there were always dogs.

When out prowling Bryna would always investigate the slightest signs of other cats

– just in case – sniffing out a day-old scent that still clung to the air, or chasing the wind for a tuck of cat's fur freshly pulled out upon the wire of a garden fence; but it never came to anything.

Sometimes, through the still of a windless night, they would hear the sound of cats crying. Or worse, the dreadful noise of a cat and a dog in a street fight, their voices carrying far out across the town.

"Listen to that, just listen," Treacle said, huddling closer to Bryna.

"Shh. Shh— you'll only wake Crumpet." Bryna watched the young mother as she lay fretting in an uneasy sleep. Crumpet began to mew, as if in answer to the noises of the night; calling to her dead kits, as she turned and twisted ceaselessly. From somewhere, a lone cat shrieked above the rest only to be suddenly silenced. Crumpet started awake, her eyes glaring wide open. She began to search frantically, as if she did not see Bryna or Treacle there. And then she closed her eyes again.

"I can't stand much more of this," Treacle said. "It's just not a natural way to live. When are the people coming back, Bryna? Do you think it's soon?"

Before Bryna could answer, Lodger's head appeared in the entrance of their lodge. He pushed his way inside and dropped the warm body of a sparrow onto the floor. "Not moanin' again, are we? Some cats don't know when they're well off." He pawed the bird towards them. "Well, get it down you, won't keep forever. I'm not that hungry myself." With that he turned and went out again, his raggy old tail flicking a quick goodbye behind him.

Crumpet stirred herself again at the smell of food and so, as best they could, they shared the bird between them. It was a brief comfort. The tug at the belly, the sharp sourness that filled the mouth, the joyous burn in the nose was all too much for such a miserably small dinner. First Treacle and then Crumpet followed Lodger out into the darkness.

Only Bryna did not hunt that night. She stayed inside the iron drum and slept, and while she slept she had a dream. A bad dream.

A nightmare . . .

A dark shadow crept out of the wild, and came down into the town. What it was, who it was, there was no telling. Shapeless and nameless, old beyond age, it stalked the streets. And where it stalked, it killed. It killed cats. It killed dogs. And when its killing was done the shadow was gone, and the nightmare went with it.

Bryna woke up with a start. It was early morning. Treacle was curled up comfortably asleep at her side. But Lodger was sitting upright and alert, just beyond the entrance of their lodge.

"What is it?" Bryna asked.

Lodger's ears twitched awkwardly, as if he had been listening very hard for something and she had broken his concentration. "The young mother, Crumpet, she has not returned from her prowl. It is not like her to stay away so long."

Lodger waited there in silence all that day. At nightfall, he went in search of her, only to return again hours later, on his own.

Crumpet did not come back on that second night.

Crumpet did not come back.

Thirteen

DROWNING

"It's raining, Bryna. Hurry, wake up! It's raining." Treacle's mew was desperate. "Wake up, will you?" He nipped and tugged at Bryna's fur with his teeth.

"Ow! What rain?" Bryna opened one eye and thrust it accusingly at the kit. She had been in the middle of another dream. Only this time it had been a dream of home and Mrs Ida Tupps. There had been warm firesides, soft sofas and long cat-naps. And there had been food – there had been lots and lots of food – any time she mewed for it. "You've woken me up to tell me about rain!" Her claws scratched at the rusted iron of the oil drum, making it vibrate. The whole lodge seemed to shake with her annoyance. "Why won't you ever let me sleep?" She wanted to spit curses at him, to cuff him about the ears. But she didn't. Treacle's eyes were wide open with terror.

"There's too much of it," he said, his voice thin and scared.

"*Too much?* What do you mean?" She began to sit up. "If it's really raining, then it will wash away all this rotten snow, and there'll be no more winter."

"N-no. You don't understand. It's raining too much. There's been too much snow, and now there's too much rain with too much water. It's already taken Lodger."

"*Taken Lodger?* But—"

"Yes. Yes. He wasn't quick enough! It picked him right up off his paws and ran away with him. Oh, come and see. Come and see." He tugged at her fur again, let go, and darted outside.

"Oh, all right. I'm coming. But if this

is another silly game . . ." Bryna stretched, stood up slowly and sulkily, and followed him outside.

The rain was falling hard and cold, and very fast. Great twisting black sheets of water curled menacingly across the late afternoon sky. It caught in her fur, instantly making tats of it, leaving her looking as if some animal had chewed her up in its mouth. On the ground the deep snow drifts were dissolving around her almost as she watched.

"See! *See!*" Treacle cried, running to the very edge of the riverbank. "There's too much water, too much—" The hiss and roar of rain and river carried his voice away.

And then, as Bryna tried to make sense of it all, there was water coming up as well as coming down. The river came scrambling over its banks, rushing greedily towards the rubbish tip, and Treacle was screaming and flailing about upon his back. An instant later, Bryna wasn't standing up any more. Instead she was spinning, around and around, and the rainswept air was suddenly very thick and heavy. It gurgled and rippled and bulged with dirt-grey muscles that turned her over, and over again, in its massive arms. It paralysed her – like a kit picked up in its mother's mouth – tossed her, dragged her, pushed her mercilessly wherever it liked. And worse, it smothered her, filled her nose and mouth, and stole away her breath. Wrapped her up tight in its solid deathly coldness.

The water suddenly threw her upwards, and for one brief moment she was floating on its surface. There in front of her was Treacle, or at least something that looked like it had once been Treacle . . . but then it wasn't Treacle, only their iron drum – their lodge – bobbing madly about. It turned over, belching out great mouthfuls of air as if it was breathing its last breath, and then it sank.

Bryna was pulled down again, deep into the water, thrown forwards, turned over, thrown forwards again. She felt her body catapulted against some hard object. Felt the stabs of pain as it struck out, like the claws of some terrible unseen enemy, cutting her, tearing her, breaking her. Then she was pushed forward again, and – inseparable now – her enemy moved with her.

Lifted and dashed. Pulled. Pushed. Turned over. Turned over again. And never a breath. Never, never, never a breath.

Drowning. Drowning . . .

It was still raining. Bryna could sense the drops of water pat-a-patting upon the ground around her. It was a lighter rain now, almost soothing, and not cold exactly. She was too numb to feel cold. Inside her ears, inside her eyes, inside her nose and mouth there was the river – its taste, its smell, and its terror. They all lingered, and reminded.

She tried to make some sense out of what had happened, but could find no sense in it. Bryna knew nothing of man-made flood barriers. Barriers that were supposed to be closed in times of heavy rain to protect the town and its bridge from flood water. Barriers that stood gaping wide open.

She felt the urge to run away from the river. But no. No. Why should she run? She did not want to run. Not ever again. Did not want to move. Did not want to know at all . . .

When she woke the second time it had stopped raining. She was still blinded, and deafened, but she felt the coldness now, and it hurt. She hurt. And the coldness and the hurt were everything. If she did not move now . . . If she did not move now, she would never move again.

She tried to open her eyes, but was stopped by a pain that drove sharpened claws deep into her head. Instead, she pushed out her tongue and brushed her face and whiskers against the ground, and against the stiff coldness that was her body. Somehow she had become twisted up, was the wrong way around. Back to front. And she was stuck. Trapped, like there was something else there with her keeping a tight hold. There was a body, and there were legs. But surely they couldn't all be her legs. She began to panic. Was she still bound up with that strange water enemy, even as it lay dead? She tried to move one of the legs, to touch it. There were no claws, no teeth to bite with. No body at all. Just a piece of wood, the branches of a tree, just an ancient piece of storm-bound drift wood.

Move Bryna. Move now.

Inch by inch she worked herself free. Paw over paw. Pulling herself forwards, just to slip backwards again when her weakened body would not support her. Blindly scratching for a hold among coarse sands, then gravel, then clattering pebbles.

Then there was a steep barrier, where heavy, wet, pungent grass mingled with the sodden soil, and fell in upon itself as her claws reached out among it.

Another inch. Another paw. Pulling herself across the muddy ground. Never knowing where she was, or where she was going.

She fell in among another tangle, felt the pull of something tightening around her, something that reminded her strangely of Mrs Ida Tupps' woolly cardigans and wet newspaper. But there was a warmth there too, and she knew she had done with struggling.

Fourteen

BEACON AND A TRICKY KNOT

"Well, well, what have we got here? A pussy cat. With a collar and a name-tag and everything. Now then, is it a Tiddles or a Dribbles, a Fluffy-kins or a Kitty-witty?" Bryna was asleep and the voice seemed to drift about comfortably inside her head. "And I thought I'd maybe found myself breakfast." The voice laughed with a deep tak-ak, tak-ak.

Bryna started awake, blinking her eyes until they cried with the pain. "Treacle—?" There was a large blurred face staring down at her. "Treacle, is that you?" She blinked again through the pain, but the face stayed blurred. She tried to sit up instead, but her movement brought only more pain and was met by a crackle and a clack. She was caught fast in another trap.

"You've got yourself into a proper pickle, lass," the voice said. "I think papers is for reading, and balls of wool is maybe's for knitting or tying up parcels, but neither's for pussy cats." The voice tak-aked with laughter.

"Paper? Wool?" Bryna began to remember. "The-the water was rising . . . the river was flooding . . . Where's Treacle and Lodger? I've got to find them." She tried to sit up again.

"Hold still, lass. There's no point in you struggling. You're just one big tangle of pussy cat. If you're wanting out, I'll have to do it." A broad flat paw, with claws drawn out, sliced through the strands of wool in a series of short, easy strokes. The paper fell away with it and Bryna plopped free like a pea bursting out of its pod. Released from the stranglehold, her legs simply ignored her command to stand up and she collapsed in a heap on the ground. And with her release came the rest of the pain. A sudden, brutal pain, shooting everywhere all at once.

"OOWWwww . . ." she squealed.

"For pity sakes, lass. You'll be giving me deaf. You're alive, aren't you?" the voice said coldly. "You beat that flood didn't you? I don't know how you did it, but you did. So you're not going to die of a few busts and bruises."

"OOWWwww!" Bryna cried out again, deliberately loud. Slowly, she turned her head and tried to focus properly on the cat's face in front of her. The face stayed obstinately blurred. But there was something familiar about it all the same . . . something about its size that made her remember a garden, and a dead bird, and another strange cat who had called her names. "Grundle—?" she began.

Tak-ak, tak-ak, the cat laughed. But it was

a laugh with a hole in it, not sounding quite right, as if it was really a question. "Grundle, do you say?" the cat laughed again. "That's some name for a house-cat to be throwing about." She stopped laughing and licked her front paw thoughtfully. "Well, I'm no Grundle. My name's Beacon," and she added as an afterthought, "welcome stranger."

Bryna did not answer her. Instead she decided that, pain or no pain, this time she really was going to stand up.

"Hang on – you'll be doin' for yourself." Beacon threw herself at Bryna, knocking her back to the ground.

"Miaow!" Bryna tried to turn from under her attacker, to find ears with her teeth.

"Can't you see! Can't you see at all!" Beacon cackled. "There's a ruddy great river right there in front of you. And if you don't start behavin' yourself I'll bite your ruddy head off. You see if I don't." Beacon used the whole weight of her body, in an easy practised way, pinning Bryna where she lay.

Bryna could only cry and spit, and wait for the blows she was sure would follow. She was right, only they weren't quite the blows she was expecting; the scuff was soft and damp and . . . and . . . Beacon was washing her. Licking and pawing, cleaning her up, just like a tiny kit. "MiaOW! OW! My eyes! That hurts!" Bryna cried, embarrassed, flustered.

"Of course it hurts – there's river and muck and blood and all sorts in them eyes of yours. And if you don't stop wriggling about I'll never get them clean."

"OW!" Bryna cried again, but she gave in to the indignity of the wash. Her eyes stung worse than ever as the wild cat worked her tongue and closed paw across her face. Piece by piece, fragments of something hard and dry began to break off and were washed away, and slowly, very slowly . . . Bryna began to see again.

First there was Beacon. She was all pink tongue, and great big glowing green eyes, eyes far too big for her head (even though it was at least twice the size of Bryna's). The rest of her was far less impressive. Her fur was an indistinct muddy colour, and her body – though heavy and muscular – was squat and ugly. But those eyes . . . she was well-named.

After Beacon there was the soggy newspaper and the tats of wool. Somehow, during the storm-flood, it had all been caught in a hollow on the wire roots of a broken concrete fence post. It had wrapped itself so successfully around her during the night it had left her trussed up like a parcel, kept her warm, saved her life even. It was all shreds now where Beacon's claws had cut it to pieces.

After the paper and the wool and the fence root, there was just the river. To her horror Bryna discovered she really was sitting on the very edges of its southern bank. A steep, new bank, cut out of the land by the flood water. She had been going to walk right off the edge when Beacon had pinned her to the ground. The wild cat too had saved her life.

Bryna looked down into the waters of the river. It was so calm, so quiet now. Just like it had always been, its water gently tickling the rocks and plants in its shallows as it passed by. Had there really been a great storm, the wild beast of a flood?

Oh, yes . . . It had taken Bryna to its very heart. Dragged her from one bank, and spat her out again upon the other bank. And where the flood beast had risen it had devoured. In front of her a bridge had been bitten clean in two. Where the crumbs of its stonework had fallen, a broken line of rocks – like a giant's stepping stones – lay across the water. Where there should have been a huge mountain of rubbish, and an old iron oil drum tipped on its side, there was nothing. Just nothing. In the water the odd leg of a chair, or plastic bag, or cardboard soap box tipped and ducked, bobbed and bopped like so many drowned animals.

"Treacle!" Bryna suddenly cried out. "Treacle?"

She would have been in the water this time, if Beacon hadn't knocked her down again.

"There's nowt to find out there lass, nowt but muck and dead bodies," and then more gently, "and no way back for you either. Least ways, not 'til you get your strength back; you'd not get halfway across those fallen rocks. Come on, let's see if we can't get those legs of yours working. There's some family of mine who'll just be dying to see that pretty collar of yours . . . And we might find something to eat while we're about it."

Fifteen

THE HOLE IN THE TOWN

Beacon led Bryna away from the swollen
river. They moved uphill, always uphill,
through a pickle of streets, gardens and
back lanes almost identical to those on
her own side of the river. Until that is,
the buildings suddenly stopped. In front
of them opened up a huge, gaping green
space. A hole in the town full of . . . full of
nothing to Bryna's eyes. The green was the
green of grass. It was as if all the gardens
in all the town had been joined together in
one place. Here and there a tarmac lane had
been allowed to cut across it, following the
broken lines of ancient hedgerows. And at
its edges there ran an endless barbed-wire

fence that seemed to be trying to keep the rest of the town out.

"What is it?" Bryna gasped, refusing to move another step. "What have they done with all the houses?"

Beacon began to purr with laughter, but seeing Bryna's worried face, thought better of it and instead said gently, "That's fields, lass. You know, just fields. It's called the Town Moor . . . Come on, it's dinner-time." She set off confidently across the open grass. "Come on."

Still Bryna refused to move. There were huge four-legged beasts lolloping about the open fields of the Town Moor. Beasts with legs as thick as lampposts, and big patches of black-and-white hair splashed across their massive bodies that seemed to blot out the daylight. Their smell was heavy and stale, but strangely sweet at the same time. And there was another puzzle; these were not wild animals, but not pets either. No, something far more worrying . . . animals resigned to their fate. They all stood, heads in the grass, jaws endlessly chewing, their enormous brown eyes gawping ahead of them without interest. Bryna had smelt their scent often enough on a night wind, but somehow had never quite believed in them. They were the strange giants of old cat's tales, whose only desire in life was to offer themselves up as food for men. Could there really be such an animal?

But if the animals weren't worrying enough, there was something else. Standing further off, there were trees. Not small, sensible, garden-sized trees, standing prettily on their own; but huge great tall trees as big as buildings, and all packed tightly together in one great lump. Like an army. And there was a second barbed-wire fence, wrapped tightly around them, as if it was trying desperately to hold them all together.

"Oh, come on . . ." Beacon cried out, "cattle don't bite, and neither do the trees of a wood. At least not the ones I've ever met." As she spoke she circled around and behind Bryna, and gently bullied her forwards across the open fields.

Beacon kept bullying until she had brought Bryna to the very edges of the trees. There was a series of low buildings hidden in among the outer fringes of the wood. The wild cat encouraged Bryna to take water from a shallow wooden trough that leant against the gable wall of a small stone-built house. "This here's what's called a farmyard," said Beacon. "And that there's what's left of the chickens." She nodded towards some dried-up brownish-black stains that spattered the concrete yard and the wooden gate of the farmhouse garden. "It were the dogs who had the most of them, lass. All in one go too. Greedy beggars." There were stains, and there was a peculiar smell – the petrified death smell – heavy with panic and fear, and . . . and there were the thinnest of grey shadows strutting backwards and forwards across the yard. Bryna felt her fur stiffen across her back, and strangely, saliva began to drip from the corner of her mouth.

"Can't eat ghosts, lass," said Beacon. Bryna stared at her in wonder.

"Then, then you can see them too? I knew there were others, but—"

"Me? Oh no, lass, no, not me. Right down to earth I am. Got myself the sharpest pair of eyes in the whole world, but I only see things that are really there."

"Then, then how did you know?"

"I know a spooked cat when I'm looking at one. And anyway, it doesn't take much guessing," she laughed, almost mockingly. "You called out Grundle's name when we first met, like you knew him. Like you knew him special."

"But I, I did. I do – sort of."

"Ha! Well, there you are then. He's been dead these last four seasons. Aye, dead. Long before you were even a twinkle in the eye of some dirty old tom cat. And I should know. Grundle was *my* mate. Come on, let's go and pay him a visit."

Bryna licked her haunches, frantic with shame and embarrassment. "He was *so* real. Not just shadows, like these chickens." She stopped licking, and eyed Beacon suspiciously. "But if you know he's dead, how are you taking me to see him?"

Beacon laughed again. "I'll leave that for you to work out yourself." She ducked under the wire boundary fence and disappeared in among the trees.

"Wait, please, I don't understand . . . And I don't like all these trees so close together. It's not natural." Reluctantly Bryna followed Beacon under the wire, kept her backside firmly in sight, and tried to ignore the way the wood seemed to close in around her, cutting out what little winter light there had been.

* * *

"Grundle," Beacon mewed softly. "Grundle, here's a friend to see you." Bryna's ears stood up on end. She tried to use her eyes to focus upon the dead, and stanced herself for the shock of pain that would fill her head as the ghost appeared . . . Nothing happened. There were just trees, and the shadows of trees, and something lying, entangled in the grass close to where Beacon now stood. It was a skull, a cat's skull, large and broad, and still armed with a terrifying pair of fangs that seemed to bite into the ground where it rested. For all that, it was just an empty skull. There were no eerie phantoms. It was nothing more than a cat's waymark now. Bryna stayed silent, unsure of what was expected of her. Beacon stared at the skull, lost for a moment somewhere in the past, and then she began to laugh, "I expect he's lost a bit of weight since you last saw him." Bryna laughed too – only to find their laughter split by the rude cackle of a new voice.

"Mother – what *have* you brought back with you this time?" A sleek black cat, a young, full-grown female, stepped out of the shadows of the trees. "This is a house-cat," she protested loudly, eyeing Bryna with a mixture of contempt and barely disguised ridicule.

Bryna opened her mouth to argue only to be beaten to it by Beacon's snarling mew. "Dart, use your eyes. Can't you see the sorry state she's in? Or would you have had me leave the lass to die where I found her?" Beacon glared at her daughter.

Bryna opened her mouth again. Wanted to say she had not been about to die. And that anyway, even if she *had* been about to die, she could look after herself!

"But a *pussy*-cat!" snarled Dart, her fur beginning to bristle, "a *pet*." She threw out the last word like she was sicking up a hair-ball. The tails of both cats lifted and twitched, signalling their anger.

Bryna felt sure she should be joining in,

taking a bite out of *some* cat. She never got the chance, because just then, from out across the open fields behind the trees, there came a long low triumphant howl. Then there were growls and snarls, and the yap-yapping of a sudden pursuit.

"Dogs," spat Dart. "Bloody dogs on to a scent." She instantly forgot her argument with her mother and stared accusingly at Bryna as if it was somehow her fault.

"They're out on the hunt again," said Beacon. "Now that their human nursemaids have disappeared. Now that there is nothing left for them to scavenge from their dirty streets and smelly dustbins."

Again Dart looked accusingly at Bryna. "And I know exactly who they'll be hunting—" Without finishing she took off with a bounding leap, disappearing into the trees at a speed Bryna had never seen in a cat before. Dart, like her mother, was well-named.

"You must forgive my daughter's anger.

146

It's just her way, lass," Beacon said. "But be certain of this – if there's trouble heading our way, she'll be the first to see it off." Beacon lifted her head and sniffed at the air anxiously. "Come, quickly, follow me, they are getting close." At that Beacon launched herself up the nearest tree. Its trunk was as straight as a lamppost and had no branches within a cat's leap, and yet with seeming ease she clawed her way up to its highest branches. There she squatted, the muddy-grey colours of her fur a natural camouflage against the bark.

"Come on then—"

Bryna tried to follow. She leapt at the tree. Her claws struck the bark, held there for a moment, only to tear free again, sending her sprawling to the ground.

The howling of the dogs sounded very near now. Perhaps even within the woods. The heavy dog scent began to foul the air. Bryna jumped at the tree again, made an extra stride, then two, just to fall back again.

"I can't climb it. I can't," she whined, her eyes searching for an easier way of escape. The undergrowth was thin and uneven. There was nowhere to run but up.

"Have you forgotten all that is your nature? You're nobody's pet now, lass," Beacon hissed. "You're a cat. A ruddy wild cat. So jump with all your heart. Jump for all your life's worth."

The cries of the dogs filled Bryna's head. They were so close now she could almost tell one bark from another. Frantic, Bryna turned a full circle, took a run, and leapt. Leapt for her life. Up she went, and this time she did not stop.

"Lay yourself out flat, lass. Say nowt, watch carefully and stay out of sight," Beacon said, pulling the frightened cat down across her branch. An instant later Dart burst out of the undergrowth and sped past their tree at full flight. Charging after her, almost on her tail, came a huge Great Dane. Further off, to her left and to her right, there were other dogs – unseen as yet, but their smells unmistakeable – shadowing her mercilessly.

"We must get down. We must help her," Bryna hissed.

Beacon reached out a paw and gripped Bryna by the scruff of the neck. "No, lass. You stay where you are." She was purring quietly to herself. "It's Dart who is helping us."

And so they lay, and waited. Slowly, agonisingly slowly for Bryna, the sounds of the chase began to fade into the distance. Just as the noises faded away completely Bryna suddenly realised – although she was sure she had never taken her eyes off the ground – there was a cat sitting quietly at the base of the tree. A tom, not big, but a full-grown sleek-furred ginger. He looked strangely familiar, except . . . except she knew she had never seen this cat before. His front left leg was missing from paw to knee, but it was an old injury; his fur had grown neatly over the stump disguising the worst of the wound.

And then Dart was at the stranger's side. "Ki-ya, my brother, you are safe." She licked frantically at his face as if he was her kit, before suddenly remembering Bryna. She turned away from him and scowled up at the tree tops. "Here, kitty-kitty," she said, mockingly. "You can come out now."

PART THREE

Dread Booga looked about its dark pit, awake now. Gently stroked the bones of its long-dead mate, and remembered loneliness.

Then it felt the pain of hunger biting at its belly, and that other thing; that strange, pulsating force that burned between its fingers. Its injured head made no sense of either, but at least the dead weight of men's thoughts was gone.

Nervously, the creature began to look for a way out of the darkness . . .

Sixteen

LIVING WITH THE WILD CATS

In the days that followed Bryna changed. Beacon and her full-grown offspring, Dart and Ki-ya, fed her on meat that was freshly caught; the young of a strange long-eared animal that was almost as big as she was. "Rabbit," Beacon called it. "We'll show you how to catch your own, lass. Once you get your strength back." And her strength did come back, and old wounds healed. And somehow, the freedom, the fright of life lived hand-to-mouth – even after the dogs, and her time spent with Lodger in the iron drum – seemed to bring her more alive. More alive than she had ever known.

They lived among the trees, in roughly

hollowed-out earth dens, or under ancient fallen tree-trunks; even in the treetops themselves when needs be. Wherever suited, wherever came to hand.

Each cat spent much of its time alone, coming together only to hunt, to talk, or, more rarely, when there was a need for those still times of quiet companionship.

Outwardly Dart never softened towards Bryna. Always protective of her younger brother she would mock and skit the house-cat endlessly. But Dart was always the first there when help was needed. Always the first to the hunt, and the first to return triumphant. And always – however grudgingly – always willing to share her kill.

The three younger cats took to prowling together. Not in a tight pack, but at a distance, keeping only within earshot of each other. Dart would always be off ahead somewhere.

"I can't wait around for invalids and useless

amateurs. We'd get nothing to eat all night,"
she'd moan, giving Bryna filthy looks, before
running off on her own through the wood. It
was then that Ki-ya would turn his head oddly
on its side, and the sound of his deep gentle
purr would rise up in his throat, as if he was
saying *Don't mind her, don't mind her.*

Ki-ya had only three legs but he was far
from being slow; his speed and guile at the
hunt was only just short of his sister's. It
was Bryna who always found herself trailing
last. In the early days she would sometimes
lose their scents among the trees and in a
state of panic break cover and come chasing
wildly after them. And then around some
tree or in some hollow she would find herself
bumping awkwardly into Ki-ya. Always Ki-ya.
He would be faking a limp, or listening to
some sound that she couldn't hear, sniffing
at some scent that never quite reached her
nose: pretending he was not waiting there
for her to catch him up.

And if he was not slowed up by his lack of legs, neither was his art at the kill any the less. He found it as easy to bring down a young rabbit at full stretch with his one front paw, as Bryna found it almost impossible with her two. "Perhaps I should bite off one of your paws, pussy," Dart skitted. "Then maybe's you'd hunt as well as my brother here."

Bryna might have turned on her, but for Ki-ya's soft purr gently calling, *"Don't mind her. Don't mind her."* Instead, she lifted a front leg and began hobbling about on three paws, pretending to chase awkwardly after an invisible rabbit. She tumbled over, fell heavily, missed its invisible neck with a snap of her teeth, and burst out laughing. Then Ki-ya and Dart played copycat and threw themselves after her, mewing like silly kits, stretching themselves out carelessly under the afternoon sun.

For now there were no more dogs, no more ghosts or bad dreams, and for Bryna that was enough.

Seventeen

THE SHADOW STALKING

"What was it really like, lass – living with them?" Beacon asked one evening as the four cats lazed away a warm spring evening, belly-full and content after a successful hunt.

"Them?" said Bryna.

"You know, *people.*"

"Oh yes, come on, tell us all about it. What was it like living in a house?" Ki-ya said enthusiastically, licking the last spot of warm rabbit's blood from the end of his nose.

"Pah! Who wants to know that?" said Dart. She tucked her tail in under her chin, half-closed her eyes, and lay watching her younger brother and the house-cat Bryna. Watched them very carefully.

"Well, I don't know really. It was . . . it was warm," Bryna began, trying to remember how it had been. "Yes, warm, and, and closed in. It seems so very long ago now." The long afternoons spent in front of roaring fires. The easy food, and easy company. "There was Mrs Ida Tupps and me, and we had a whole house all to ourselves. I used to sleep on her knee—" (Beacon tut-tutted and looked knowingly at Dart). "There was a big box that sat on a table in the corner of the front room. Sometimes it was full of strange voices."

"Voices in a box," spat Dart, trying to sound as if she wasn't the least bit interested. "I don't believe that. Wasn't there anything proper – like other cats?"

For a moment Bryna didn't say anything. In her mind she saw the town streets again. Saw Dexter and Fat Blossom, Lodger, and poor Treacle. "It was safe inside the house . . ." she said at last, but her voice trailed off, and left behind it a chill silence.

"I talked to an old house-cat once," Beacon said, hoping to lift the mood. "He told me his people spent all of their time rubbing things with sticks. There was a stick for the floors of his house, and one for the grass in his garden. There were even short wet sticks for rubbing the walls. Always rubbing they was—"

"Well, yes, but—" Bryna tried to interrupt.

"And he said his people shed their skins every night before they slept, and grew new ones again every morning when they woke up."

Bryna tried again. "Yes, they do, but that's only clothes. That's not—"

"Mad," said Dart, "mad they are, the lot of them. No wonder they disappeared. You're much better off without them."

Bryna couldn't bring herself to argue any more. A heavy sadness had gripped her, and wouldn't let go. A sadness she could not run away from. She closed her eyes and while the voices of her companions babbled on around her she fell asleep.

And in that sleep she dreamt again. Dreamt again of dark evil things ... Of the street prowler. Of the shadow stalking. The hunter of both cat and dog, eager for the kill. Only this time she gave the creature a name, borrowed from some silly kittish memory. "Dread Booga!" she called out in her sleep. It gave her no rest. Silently, swiftly, it began to search her out, came ever closer. And she, in her turn, ran away from it. Ran wildly, and would not stop running—

A distant crack of thunder woke her with a start.

She was alone. It was the middle of the night. Her paws felt damp, the hair on her back and neck stood rigid, and a thick bile sickened her throat and soured her tongue. In her sleep she had backed herself into a hole beneath a knot of tree roots she had been sheltering against. Through the tangle of roots and the leafless, spring-budded treetops above her, she could see the sky. There was no moon, no stars. She sensed the blackened clouds that hung there, incredibly low, oppressive, and heavy. The air around her was cold to the touch of her nose; but this was not the cold of a fresh spring night.

The shadows of her dark dream still filled her head and made it ache with a steady dull pulse. She pricked up her ears and tried to listen to the night. There was nothing unusual, no more thunder . . . Perhaps, like Dread Booga, that too had been a part of her strange nightmare. Even so, she did not sleep again that night. She sat there, as still as the trees, and watched. Watched until a thin watery sun worked its way through the treetops and diluted the blackness.

With the morning came the urgent mewing of a cat.

"Bryna. Oh, Bryna, where are you, lass?

Where are you?" Beacon came bounding through the trees, her whole body heaving with excitement. "Come out. Come out and see what Ki-ya has caught for himself."

Bryna shuffled herself out through the roots of her tree, noisily rustling the carpet of dead leaves that had gathered there the previous autumn, politely signalling her presence to Beacon. (Beacon was excited enough without having her think some wild animal was creeping up on her.)

"Oh, there you are. Well, lass, you've got to come and see this for yourself." Beacon never stopped running. She flew past Bryna going one way, swung around the nearest tree and flew past her again going back the way she had come. "Never seen anything like it. Never. And with three legs too. *Three legs!*" There was nothing for Bryna to do but chase after her.

Beacon led her out of the wood, through the wire fence and on to the field beyond.

The big black-and-white gawp-eyed cattle were standing feeding, just the same as always. Bryna's ears pricked up. Ahead of her she could hear Dart and Ki-ya calling eagerly to each other.

And then she saw it, lying there upon the ground like a huge toppled mountain . . . a fallen bullock. It still stared at her gawp-eyed, but it saw nothing now. It was dead, quite dead. One side of its huge body had been torn open across its length; a wound so deep and terrible, it had taken only the one to bring the animal down. This was no cat's kill. No dog pack, either. And it wasn't dogs or cats who had eaten their fill upon the carcass. The dark shadow of another hunter clung there. And impossible though it was, Bryna knew it for the creature that had haunted her dreams. She was certain this death was Dread Booga's work.

"Well, pussy-cat, what do you think of this?" Dart cried with delight, plunging her teeth into the loose fronds of fresh red meat that trailed from the carcass, as if she had just wrestled the animal to the ground all on her own and was making the kill herself.

Ki-ya looked up from the spot where he was feeding upon a string of scattered entrails. He mewed at her joyfully, and went back to his feast.

"You made this kill?" Bryna asked anxiously.

Ki-ya lifted his head again with mock embarrassment. "Well, I might have exaggerated for my mother's sake. But I did find the beast first!"

"We won't have to hunt for days and days," Beacon said proudly, as if she hadn't heard her son's confession, and she pounced greedily upon the carcass, suddenly desperate for her share of the spoils.

Slowly and carefully Bryna approached the body of the bullock. There were strange scents hanging in the air around it. One seemed oddly familiar, but then again, not.

And something had burnt here, though there were no visible signs, something that left her nose stinging. "I-I don't like this . . . it's-it's not natural, somehow."

"Oh, pah!" spat Dart. "What more do you want? The creature's deader than a stone. It couldn't even hurt a scaredy-cat now."

"It's just that, it's just . . ." She didn't finish. It was all too hard to explain, even to herself, and her mouth was dripping with saliva as the tantalising scent of fresh meat began to mask both the smell of fear and that of the hunter.

For several days the carcass of the bullock lay in the field. It became an essential part of their daily prowl. An easy meal, and not only for the cats. Bryna caught the smell of dog on the second morning. And something else fed there too . . . something much larger, that splintered the biggest of the bones as if they were twigs, took off a whole leg at one go and carried it away. And if the scent that remained belonged to a hunter, it was something else too . . .

The smell of a bad dream. The smell of Dread Booga.

Eighteen

THE SHADOW FALLING

Then came the morning when what was left of the dead bullock was not worth eating. Its meat was too old and maggot-ridden even for the scavengers, and its scattered bones were no longer moist pink, but dry white.

The day started brightly. The sun was shining, throwing deep shadows between the trees, and there was no wind to carry a cat's scent. Perfect conditions for a hunt. Beacon led the way across the Town Moor and down on to one of the narrow lanes that would take them into the outskirts of the town and eventually to the riverside. It was a lazy prowl. Ki-ya and Dart walked side by side a few paces behind their mother, and Bryna a few paces behind them. Only instinct kept them off the tarmac road and within the shadows of the hedgerow that ran alongside the lane. There were no speeding cars or treacherous lorries threatening to run them down, but old habits die hard, and the less any likely prey knew of their presence the better.

They didn't get far. Beacon hissed at them to stop.

"What is it?" Ki-ya called, standing still.

"We must take cover. Quickly now. There's little time."

Without further question the four cats scampered up the shallow earth bank that formed the base of the hedge at the side of the lane. And one by one they found a make-shift spot to hide within it.

"What is it, Beacon?" Ki-ya called again, his eyes and ears alert and searching. His senses told him nothing, but he'd learnt to trust his mother's skills. It was a common enough routine.

"There, look – see? Where the lane twists towards the bottom of the valley. We aren't the only animals out on the prowl." Beacon's eyes were so much better than her kits it was some moments before they caught on.

"Dogs?" said Dart.

"Aye lass, dogs. Come across the river by the stones o' the old bridge. Six of them . . . although I was near certain I counted seven. And they're moving this way, very fast."

"Well, if they're after the meat of that bullock, they're wasting their time. Even their stomachs couldn't keep it down now."

"Shush – be still now."

The cats held their breath. The dogs were already getting close and a scented breath would have given them away faster than a cry. Perhaps, if they did not breathe, if they kept perfectly still, if the heads of the dogs were full up with whatever nonsense it was they were intent upon pursuing, the cats wouldn't be noticed there, hidden in the shadows of the hedge.

The dog pack didn't break its pace. Soon it would be past. Soon they would be safe.

A terrier at the back of the pack suddenly skidded awkwardly, lost his stride, and pulled himself to a stop. He sat down heavily, self-consciously, used a back leg to scratch away a fly he pretended was bothering his ear.

The cats froze. Or at least, they thought they did. The dog stood up again, held his head high. His wet nostrils twitched, strained, searched the air for something.

"Come on, Yip-yap," barked an ugly brown-haired mongrel at the front of the pack. "Stop messin' about."

Yip-yap started at the sound of his name. Sniffed the air again, and then, wagging his short stub-end of a tail, bounded after his companions.

"That was a close call," whispered Bryna. "Too close."

"I reckon we could have handled them, if we'd had to," Dart said, weakly, her voice giving away the pretence in her words.

"Shush!" hissed Beacon. "It's not over yet, lass. There's still one missing. I'm certain of it." Ki-ya sensed his mother's nervous mood. If there was no wind to carry away a cat's scent, there was no wind to bring a dog's scent to them.

"GOTCHA!" roared Khan. The huge dog charged at them from behind, came straight at them through the thickest part of the hedge, eyes glaring, teeth bared.

There was instant panic, instant movement. The cats shot out from beneath the hedge, with nowhere to run but out into the middle of the lane. Bryna found herself facing the dog pack. It had turned around in response to Khan's excited outburst.

The stench of the dogs, their hot, panting breath, engulfed her. At first her paws flailed about uselessly as their mass of heavy bodies turned and twisted around and over her, agitated to the attack. Snarls, roars, squeals of pain, all became the same then. Ki-ya's head appeared for a moment over the back of a poodle, only to disappear again as Dart shot out from between the legs of the ugly mongrel. And then, suddenly, a flash of Beacon's claws—

The dogs may have had the element of surprise, but they were not quite prepared for a fight with wild cats. Bryna began to find her mark. She struck out instinctively with open claws, planted them deep: found fur, or skin, or muscle, anything that gained her a hold. Then she pushed out with her back legs in an attempt to throw herself upwards and clear of the pack. She would have made it too, if Yip-yap hadn't been turning in mid-air, attempting to bite off Beacon's tail as it whipped passed him. Dog and cat collided, and landed together in a heap.

Yip-yap was quick enough to catch hold of Bryna's ear in his teeth, tearing it to shreds like a piece of soggy newspaper. Fortunately for Bryna the momentum of their fall kept them rolling, and finding himself turning underneath her, Yip-yap let go for an instant. His jaws quickly snapped shut again searching for her neck and a grip he knew would bring death. But his break of hold was decisive. As Yip-yap moved, so did Bryna. She strummed frantically at his unprotected belly with her back legs. And as her claws tore open the soft flesh, they gained a firm hold there. Again instinct told her to use her advantage and throw herself clear. To run. To run and run and run.

Yip-yap was at her heels. The heat of his anger, the agony of his belly wound as much his weapons as the snap of his teeth.

"You can't run forever, cat," he yelled. Bryna's eyes stared blankly ahead, seeing nothing but escape. She did not know there

were cats running with her. Ahead of her
Dart was drawing off the main pack of dogs
with Khan at their head. Almost alongside
her ran Beacon and Ki-ya.

"She'll run you to your grave, dog," Ki-ya
hissed at the terrier.

"Aye, she will, lad. If I don't get to you
first." Beacon ran a tight circle around the
stump of an old tree. To his dismay, Yip-yap
found the wild cat charging at him from
the side, slashing at his snout with open
claws. And he was tiring now, as the pain
of his wound bit deeper. Yip-yap dropped
to the ground, turned his attack to defence
before the cat could land another blow. For
a moment Beacon was undecided; should
she try to finish off the stricken dog or
make her own escape? In front of her Dart
was losing ground to Khan, had somehow
been turned and was running into the path
of the fleeing Ki-ya and Bryna. A second
encounter with the pack would leave them

without the strength for flight. It would be all or nothing.

The dogs began to bay and howl as they were filled with the madness of the hunt.

But the real madness was only just beginning.

In a single moment the chase was suddenly ended. Not by a dog. Not by a cat, either. They all stood heavily upon the open ground, solid and unmoving, like lumps of stone. Pursuers and pursued. All staring in the same direction. All disbelieving what it was they saw standing there.

The creeping shadow of Bryna's nightmares began to fill her mind again. But the nightmare was not inside her head this time: it was out there in front of her. Out there in the open. Standing looking down upon them all. And its presence hurt.

Still no animal moved. Dogs and cats alike stood panting nervously, or whining, or silently crying. Puzzled beyond puzzlement.

All eyes carefully watching as the creeping shadow began to move among them.

"It's a . . . it's a man," cried out Yip-yap.

"Yes. Yes . . . it *is* a man," Bryna answered. "It *is* a man!" And yet, if this was a man, what was the shadow that hung so closely about him, disguising his form? The shadow that even now was getting darker as he approached. A clawing hurt inside Bryna's head gripped tighter, and would not let go.

"They've come back. They've come back for us!" Dogs began to bark loudly with excitement. "Yes, oh yes! Just like you said they would, Khan. Just like you said." Their tails thrashed and whipped with joy. And almost as one they began to run towards the solitary figure.

Bryna felt split in two. She too should run to greet him. Turn belly up, play begging-kitten. A strange excitement began to burn

176

deep down inside of her, tempting her forward. Tempting her even as the claws of the shadow held her back. He would be her comfort – just as Mrs Ida Tupps had been – he would feed her, keep her warm and safe . . .

Then came the roar of thunder.

Ki-ya, Beacon and Dart lay silently among the grass. They did not see dark shadows, only an animal. An animal that stood upright upon two legs. They felt no excitement at the approach of this strange, grey, gnarl-skinned creature. Only apprehension, distrust and fear: that simple, inbred fear that told them of all dangers. Its presence was enough to hold them to the ground, to make them instinctively hide themselves away, in the hope that hiding would be enough to save them.

Thunder roared again, lightning was thrown carelessly about the sky, and the creature began to cry out loud. But even as the claws of the shadow held her mind, Bryna knew enough to wonder. Surely this thunder was all wrong? Can it thunder without clouds, when the skies are clear blue? And what was the sour reek, like some foul thing burning, that came with it and stung her nose? It was as if the thunder and the lightning were coming from *inside* the man. Somehow the thunder *was* the man.

And then, at last, Bryna saw the truth of it. Saw through the shadows as the figure cried out again, like a man. *Like* a man. *Not* a man. Not quite tall enough, not quite straight enough. Too frail-looking somehow; the shallow features of its face hardly hinted at. And a deep, a terrible scar disfigured its head; long since healed over, it pulled the skin too tightly across the bones of its skull.

And if the shadow-hunter was not a man . . . what was it?

Dread Booga had stepped out of Bryna's

dreams. And if death ever stood upon two legs, this creature was it.

For a third time, lightning flashed and thunder roared, and the dogs ran on and on. Khan was almost upon the Booga, bounding gleefully, barking with joy. Heedless of the truth he could not see before him, of the terrifying noise and blinding light.

He did not take another step. His body fell heavily at the Booga's feet and did not move again.

Dread Booga squealed, not with delight, but with a kind of anguish, of fear even.

The dog pack stopped running, stood transfixed. They could not run away, or use their voices to plead.

Then another uncontrolled squealing flash, another bang. And a strange laughter mixed with even stranger words, came from the mouth of the Booga. If there was any meaning to it, it was beyond the sense of any animal there. "Etsa clow es, sai for ma I—"

Crack! "—Pro farr a? Pro farr a?" Crack! Crack! Crack!

Out across the Town Moor a Great Dane fell over and lay quite still; then another dog, and then another. Each of them dropped without so much as a whimper.

And if among it all no animal saw the streak of light that fell clumsily between the Booga's unpractised fingers, scorching the grass, turning poor Beacon's body from under her, it's little wonder. Sadly, not even Beacon's own eyes were sharp enough for that.

When, at last, the thunder fell silent the Booga lifted up Khan's body. Not yet frozen in death, the dog's mouth snapped open and shut, open and shut as the creature moved, as if even now – in death – he was calling out to the Dread Booga.

But this was not the worst of it. The Booga stooped down a second time and lifted up the smaller body of a cat. A cat whose markings were burned black and unrecognisable. With that, it began to stalk towards the heart of the town, its long, clumsy legs jarring its body like a bag of loose bones as it moved across the open ground . . .

Long, long after the Booga had gone there was a deathly still upon that Moor. Nothing moved. Nothing dared move.

Maybe they were all dead, thought Bryna. The whole world had gone mad, and they were all dead. And death was a place. Yes, of course, they were dead. Why else would Grundle be standing over her now? And there too was Dexter with Fat Blossom at his side, looking anxiously on.

But she was not dead. The shadows inside her head began to lift, the ghosts faded away and became a living dog. A shivering, cowering dog, trailing blood as it moved – but no less a real live terrier for that. Yip-yap dragged himself slowly past her without a look in her direction.

Ki-ya and Dart found Bryna there, and led her away to safety.

Not Beacon though. There was no more Beacon.

Nineteen

THE FIELD OF STONES

How many times over the next days and weeks did Bryna's mind turn back to her old life with Mrs Ida Tupps? Where all was order, changeless and sure. Where meal followed sleep followed meal as certain as night followed day. Where death did not come stalking in disguise, and if there were enemies to avoid you knew who they were.

The streets, the gardens, the roads, the riverside paths, and the open fields of the Town Moor became deserted. Dogs and cats alike, too scared to move, hid themselves away. Stayed out of sight. Only when an empty belly cried louder than the roaring thunder that haunted them all did any animal chance to venture out. In the end what choice was there? They could not stay hidden forever. Even the innocent victim must eat sometime or else meet his death anyway.

When forced to the hunt animals stalked warily and silently. Never alone, but never in packs. Too conspicuous. Don't want to be conspicuous. And if old friends or kin were met upon the way, they said little or nothing to each other, and passed by hurriedly. Even where dogs and cats met, as they turned the same street corner or chased down the same quarry, no call or threat was made. Each would check themselves, turn tail and run away, or else look purposefully ahead – as if the other was invisible – and pass on.

As time passed there were those who were foolish enough to forget; but they were found out soon enough. Dread Booga always found them out. Day or night, in sleeting rain or blazing sunshine, made no difference to the

Booga. There was to be no rest from its murderous thunder. As its roar was heard across the town any animal foolish enough to be caught out in the open stanced stricken with fear, until the dreadful noise passed away. Then they would move quickly into cover, only thankful not to have been its latest victim.

For Ki-ya and Dart it was different. It was the loss of their mother that rested most heavily upon them. They spent endless hours skulking about the wood. They fretted, or stalked aimlessly from tree to tree as if they were searching for something. Something that had left an aching unfillable hole deep inside of them. Something they must surely find in the end if only they kept on looking.

And Bryna? Scared, perplexed for herself, worried for them, followed them about, like a silly lost kit.

They took to spending all their time

together and would not be parted, slept flank to flank. Bryna on one side of Ki-ya, his sister on the other. But even in sleep there was to be no escape, no rest for Bryna. Shadows still stalked in her dreams. Not Dread Booga though. No. The Booga was out there in the real world ... now it was the dead who worried her sleep. Dexter and Fat Blossom, Brindle and Maxwell, and old Lodger. At first they would simply sit and watch her. But as the nights passed, the ghosts became restless and they began to whisper urgently to one another.

"I can't hear you!" Bryna called out to them. "I can't hear what you're saying!"

"Treacle ..." Lodger seemed to say. "Treacle ..."

"What? What *are* you saying?"

"Treacle ..." repeated Fat Blossom, desperate for her to understand.

"But Treacle's dead – he's just a ghost. A ghost like you!"

"No, Bryna . . . alive . . ."

But you wake up from nightmares and dreams, don't you? And neither are true.

The days turned, but the changing seasons did nothing to lift the darkness of their mood. Poor spring became a poorer summer. All clouds and rain. The sun, when it shone at all, was too cold to warm a moggie's back.

Forever on edge, unsettled and fearful, life was one long threat. The smallest of things could spook Bryna. A windblown leaf falling from a tree, or the first splash of rain before a shower. Her fears became her frustration, turning to anger, burning her up inside. Until, at last, she could stand it no longer. She felt that if she did not just get up and *do* something she would surely burst.

"Ki-ya, I want to go and look for Treacle," she found the courage to say. For a long moment Ki-ya stared ruefully at the house-cat. In a way it did not surprise him. What, after all, had he and his sister been doing ever since the death of their mother, but brooding over a ghost?

"Treacle's gone, Bryna. Drowned," Ki-ya said simply. There was no easy way of saying dead.

"No. No, it's not true. The ghosts told me. They told me. And I'm going to find him."

"Bryna, he's dead, as dead as . . . as dead as Beacon." Ki-ya's words came slowly, as if there was something in them that he too was seeing only for the first time. Dart turned her head away, and raked the earth with her open claws.

"I had another dream—" began Bryna.

"Pah," spat Dart, "you and your ghosts and your stupid dreams. The dead are just dead and that's an end to it."

"No, there was a field, a field full of stones growing up out of the ground. They were beautiful flat stones, line upon line of them, going on for ever." She paused, expecting Ki-ya's denial or at least Dart's abuse. But there was none. "And there was a cat standing in among the stones. A small rusty-orange-and-white cat. If there was ever such a place, then that is where I will find Treacle."

"Oh Bryna, Bryna, even if he was alive, how could you possibly find this field of stones?" said Ki-ya.

"I don't know. Maybe the ghosts will show me the way. I don't know – but I must try."

"And what about Dread Booga? Have you forgotten the reek of its evil thunder? Have you forgotten Beacon so soon?"

"I don't care. I don't care!" Bryna mewed bitterly. "And anyway, I'm not asking any cat to come with me. I can take care of myself."

An angry silence filled the space between them. Tails twisted and flicked.

It was Dart who spoke next. "You don't need ghosts to show you the way to the field of stones, Bryna. I know this place."

"What?"

"I've seen it. I've been there. It's real enough . . . a place of strange feelings. A man-made place. They put things in the ground there, bury them in boxes, and then they plant the stones on top of the boxes. But they're not like trees, they never grow."

"Where is it, then? Tell me, Dart. Please, *tell me*!"

"It's on our side of the river, but deep within the town. And it's dangerous."

"Well, if you're too scared to show me the way, then I'll go alone." Bryna stood up and took off without another word, without heed of direction or threat.

Ki-ya and Dart moved cautiously along the street, keeping low and close to the garden walls of the empty houses, losing themselves in their short shadows.

Bryna was moving a little way ahead of them, lost among the same shadows.

"Of course we couldn't let her go off on her own. Even if it is a wild-goose chase," Ki-ya hissed under his breath.

"Ghosts, pah!" Dart hissed back with a look of disgust. "We aren't safe here, and it would be a lot, *lot* quicker if you let me go first. She doesn't even know where she's going."

"Shhh – or she'll hear you."

"I don't care if she does. This is foolishness, brother. She stops and worries at every turn. Follows the wrong roads, jumps over the wrong garden walls. And it's me who has to keep putting her right."

Bryna had stopped at another street corner, hesitant, desperate to find the way without help.

"Turn left, cat. Turn left," Dart spat under her breath. "And when you get to the iron gates, stop."

Bryna turned her head to the right as if she was considering something, before grudgingly moving to the left.

The heavy, black iron gates were bounded by two solid stone pillars and a wall of almost two man heights. Bryna walked deliberately past the gates – just to annoy Dart and Ki-ya – then turned around again, sat down heavily, and waited for them to catch her up.

Dart might have said something rude, but she didn't. The moment the three cats were in front of those gates their quarrel was forgotten. This was not a place for petty argument.

There before them, right in the middle of the town, behind the closed iron gates, stood the field of stones.

Bryna shuddered involuntarily. Whereas before, the unknown streets had merely smelled dangerous and forbidding, this place smelled oddly of something else, something she was never able to describe better than . . . old death. In its never-ending lines of mouldering grey-green stones, in its withering patches of overgrown grass, in its sickly, decaying, long-neglected flower borders, there was the same lingering odour. But not a scent. No. Scents come and go, windblown. This was something more; this was permanent, part of its very substance.

Against everything she knew, Bryna forced herself to stand up and edge towards the gates, just to find herself gripped by a cat's teeth and pulled back forcibly.

"There's something not right with this place, Bryna." Ki-ya's eyes were pleading.

"I didn't ask you to come," said Bryna, pulling herself free.

"It's not a place for cats," Dart cried.

"I must find Treacle." Bryna thrust her head and shoulders between the iron bars of the gate. Instantly a crowd of shadows shrouded her mind, and a blackness fell upon her as surely as if she'd been blinded.

Then there was the weight of a sudden movement at her side. And before she could find her voice to protest, Ki-ya had leapt between the iron bars, and disappeared among the lines of stones.

"Stay, Bryna," Dart snarled, forced to use her claws to hold her back. "Let him go. If there's any animal alive in this awful place then he will find it."

"But this is *my* task—"

"Stay," Dart snarled again. But then softened her voice. "We'll wait for him here, together."

They sat at that gate and listened to the silence, watched anxiously the unchanging lines of grey-green stones. Just once they caught a glimpse of Ki-ya's long ginger tail flashing between one distant stone and the next. But nothing more. So much had already disappeared from Bryna's world . . . Mrs Ida Tupps . . . Dexter . . . Treacle . . . Beacon . . . and now Ki-ya too?

And then, without warning, the worrying ghost-shadows clouding her mind were blown away. Out there, somewhere among the gravestones, a cat squalled angrily. Its shriek filled the graveyard, as it flew between the stones, chased or chasing.

"Ki-ya?" Dart and Bryna stood up together, stanced to attack. "Ki-ya, is that you?" Another squeal. Shorter, sharper than the first; a different cat. Then, before either cat could move, Ki-ya was there, coming towards them. His three-legged limp exaggerated under the weight of the load he was carrying between gritted teeth. He was pulling something along the ground, something that did not want to come with him, something that was fighting back.

He let go of his struggling baggage just in front of the iron gates. "You'd best be Treacle, for your own sake. Or I'll give you more than the back of my paw."

"S-sorry. I didn't mean—"

"Pouncing on a grown cat like that—"

There was blood.

"But nobody ever comes into the graveyard.

I–I thought you were—" Ki-ya didn't let him finish.

"I should skin you alive. If it wasn't for—"

"Treacle? TREACLE!" It was Bryna's turn to interrupt Ki-ya. "Is that *really* you? And not a ghost."

"Ghost. I should say he's not a ruddy ghost. He nearly took the back of my head off," snapped Ki-ya. "Jumping out on me like that." Treacle sprang away to the side just in case the bullying wild cat changed his mind and decided to give him a scuffing anyway. There was blood on his shoulder.

"Treacle, you're hurt," said Bryna.

"Oh no, he's ruddy well not. That's my blood—" Ki-ya started, but he shut himself up again. A strange look had come upon Bryna, a look he couldn't fathom, something that went far deeper than bruised pride. The thrum of her purr began to beat out loudly as she greeted her old friend . . .

* * *

That night there was laughter. Never in all the world could there have been four such happy cats. Finding Treacle alive seemed to breathe new life into them all. For Bryna and Treacle there was simple joy. They talked and they talked: by turns kittish, proud or boastful, happily rejoicing in the sounds of friendship. For Ki-ya and Dart a cloud had lifted, as if they too had somehow found among the gravestones something far more precious than a silly moggy. They sat silently with the house-cats, content to listen to their frivolous babble.

In truth, Bryna knew their silly words were simply filling a gap where for now they could not speak the deeper, hateful words- of tragedy that must in the end be said.

It was Bryna who talked first of Dread Booga, the creature who haunted the town, of the evil thunder and of bloody, senseless killings. But it was several more days before

Treacle finally spoke about the great flood that had brought the death of Lodger. His was a strange tale, not easily told: the words, the memories came hard to him.

"The flood took me too, Bryna . . . the water came up over my head, lifted me off my paws. Pulled me down into its depths. Drowned I was . . . good as dead . . . couldn't breathe. Choked. No air . . . I-I don't know how it was. How it happened. He was suddenly there beside me. In the water . . . He held me up. Lifted me clear." Treacle pawed the earth slowly, as if he was trying to clear away the fogginess in his head. "And then I was moving again. But not through the water this time. I thought I was flying. I could see the streets around me . . ." He fell silent again, wanted to remember properly. Wanted them to unravel the puzzle as he had done. "He carried me a long way . . . stayed with me all that night. Found us the field of stones where we could rest in safety.

No dog would bother us there. No flood could rise that far. And he had food . . ." Suddenly he turned to Bryna, his eyes wide open, stricken. "I'm not mad, Bryna. He *was* there. He *did* come for me. He did." And then his voice fell low again. "He told me we could wait together . . . for help. And we waited. I waited, Bryna, I waited for ever and ever . . . but nobody came. Nobody came!"

"What is he blithering on about?" said Dart, her bewilderment boiling over into anger. "Who is this *he*? What kind of a tom cat can do all that?"

"Don't you see at all?" said Treacle, desperate for them to understand. He stared beseechingly at Ki-ya, almost begging him to explain.

"Not a tom cat, sister," Ki-ya said slowly. "A man."

"A *man*!" Dart leapt into the air as if a man had suddenly grown up right there in front of her. "Stupid cat. There are no men, not any more. Only the Booga who stands upright on a man's legs, trying to trick us."

"No," cried Treacle. "No, not a trick. A-a *real* man." Didn't they see yet? For a moment there was complete silence. "They can come back for us . . . they can." Treacle mouthed to himself.

"Then where is he – this *real* man?" said Dart, her eyes still burning. "Did *you* see him?" she spat at her brother.

"H-h-he—" Treacle could not find his voice now.

"He is dead," said Ki-ya.

Treacle nodded, sadly.

At last Bryna began to understand. She could almost see the man at Treacle's side, could see him diving into the flood waters to pull Treacle out. Saw him huddled against the gravestones, wet and scared, his clothes sodden to the skin as he tried to keep Treacle warm through the night. She saw his body cold and stiff in the morning. And she saw his scattered remains left to rot among the grass where Ki-ya had surely come across them. There were other men dead in that place of stones, she understood that too. But, somehow, she was sure they were meant to be there. He – this other man – he had not meant to die. Not there. Not yet.

The four cats stayed close together that night, did not venture out even to find food.

As Dart fell asleep, safe and warm against her brother's flank, she thought again about the body of Treacle's strange man.

He was dead. But he was something more then dead . . . he was safe too. He was very safe. And then, in his place she saw the Booga, and slowly an idea began to form in her mind . . .

Twenty

DART'S IDEA

The following morning started with sunshine, dazzling bright in a clear blue sky. The cats found themselves coaxed to the edges of the wood by the lure of its warmth. One after another they carelessly stretched out, bathing themselves in the luxury of its heat. There wouldn't be a better time for Dart to explain her idea.

"I think . . . I think it's up to us to kill the Booga," she said quietly.

"What?"

"We must kill Dread Booga. It's the only way."

Cats' tails began to flick uneasily.

"But that's madness!" said Bryna, sitting

up, pulling Treacle up with her. "With a twist of its fingers it pulls fire from the sky and hurls death at us, and, and . . ."

"And?" said Dart.

"And we are only cats," said Treacle. "Surely it's an enemy too large and powerful to fight? Best left to itself, best avoided?"

"Avoided! *Avoided*!" stormed Dart. "There'll be plenty of time to avoid it when we're all dead. Who's been killing who?" She turned to her brother. "Eh, Ki-ya? Whose bodies are lying rotting on the streets?"

Ki-ya lay still and stayed silent, unwilling to be drawn into their argument.

"Does it hunger like us? No. Is it starving? No. Oh yes, it kills to sate its appetite, but then it kills some more. It brings us death simply because it can bring us death.

"Well, Dread Booga is not *my* master. I will not lie down and die just because it tells me to." Dart paced moodily to and fro searching for a bigger insult to throw at the house-cats. "I am not its pet. I am not its plaything. And if you only knew it – neither are you. Neither are you."

The cats turned their backs on each other and sulked. Bryna's tail flicked with confusion. Treacle washed his fur frantically, as if he could clean away the whole rotten business. But somehow Dart's idea would not go away. It felt wrong, it felt bad, and worse, it felt impossible beyond imagining. But the idea wouldn't go away.

Kill the Booga.

Kill Dread Booga and survive.

Survival? . . . Surely survival was theirs by right of nature. But . . . but . . .

"How could this be done?" said Ki-ya, breaking his silence at last, his voice calm and matter-of-fact. As if the impossible was something he did every day. Bryna stared at him in disbelief. Where had *her* Ki-ya gone? Had he caught his sister's madness? But what was worse, she found herself listening eagerly for an answer to his question.

Dart began to purr triumphantly. What better ally could she have than her own brother? "We can rid ourselves of this evil thing for good, if, *if* there are enough of us. If we take it by surprise. The streets and fields are full of cats, scared for their lives, hiding out in ones and twos. But bring them all together—"

"No, Dart." Ki-ya shook his head. "No, my sister."

Dart scowled, and for an instant Bryna brightened. Perhaps he'd come to his senses after all? But there was something strange about that *no*. It was a *no* that really meant *yes*.

"No. Cats alone cannot do this thing. No matter how great our number."

"Then how, brother? How?"

Ki-ya stood up, and turned his head towards the distant river. Sunlight played upon its surface. Bryna followed his gaze out across the town and before he could say anything more she suddenly understood what was in his mind. "The dogs," she said. "You mean the dogs, don't you?"

Treacle couldn't hide his agitation and ran and hid in the shadows of the trees. Dart shrieked with anger, and then began to laugh scathingly. "Well, pussy cat. If my idea was a madness, what is this?"

Bryna turned to look at Ki-ya. He was still looking out across the river. "I've heard it told before now that dogs have attacked men. Killed them even."

"Empty-headed dog boasts and stupid legends," said Dart. "And Dread Booga is no man!"

"Together," said Ki-ya. "Together – dogs *and* cats. One body. One strength. It might just be enough."

"Aye, might. *Might!* But dogs and cats?" Dart spat angrily. "What dog would ever kill for a cat? Or cat for a dog come to that? We'll be doing the Booga's work for it if we try that game."

"Don't you see? The Booga kills dogs just as quickly as it kills cats. They wouldn't be helping us. They'd be helping themselves. The Booga is too powerful an enemy for either cats *or* dogs on their own. And if we do nothing, then slowly, one by one, we will all surely die. This way—"

"This way death comes to us for certain," Dart spat, "but just that little bit quicker."

"*This way* there is at least a chance," said Ki-ya.

It was Dart's turn to lick at old wounds thoughtfully. "All right, supposing it might work . . . who could possibly make an alliance between a dog and a cat in the first place?"

For a long time they all fell silent, and then Bryna said quietly, "I could try."

Surely it had been a joke? Dart's idea was just

a silly piece of summer madness. Well, now it had become very real, and deadly serious, and there they were on the road, on their way to . . . *to make an alliance with a pack of dogs.* Just thinking about it sent a shiver through Bryna's body, made her tail twist and turn in the air. And had she really volunteered to do it? Even asked to go alone? One death was better than four – that's how old Lodger would have put it. Luckily for her, Ki-ya had insisted they all went with her. "At least as far as the river . . . From there Treacle and Dart can begin to round up whatever cats they can find—" There he'd paused, just as surely as if he'd added: whatever cats are crazy enough to join in such a mad scheme. Then he continued, "I'll go on with Bryna to meet with the dogs."

So, there they all were.

The riverside streets were empty and quiet. The early morning sun had failed to live up to its promise and had got lost behind clouds, leaving an odd steel-greyness about everything, making the cool summer day seem colder still. Ahead of them, lying flat and unhurried, the river cut the greyness in two with a darker, nameless colour all of its own.

Suddenly a pair of blackbirds squawked in mock fight somewhere high above them. The cats stanced low, and waited. The birds, still squawking noisily at each other, clattered their way along the gutter of a rooftop and launched themselves into the sky.

"We'll be jumping at our own shadows next,' spat Dart, with an awkward mixture of anger and embarrassment.

"Do you really think this is a good idea?" squeaked Treacle.

"Of course it isn't a good idea," said Dart, happy to find a target for her anger. "But what's that got to do with it?"

"C'mon," said Ki-ya, "we have to keep moving. We don't want to be caught out in the open when the Booga decides to take its next walk."

At the river's edge, the cats split up, without even a goodbye.

The water was low and sluggishly slow-moving. Was this really the same river that had washed away a bridge and swallowed a rubbish tip whole? Bryna stood silently on its banks. The broken image that stared back at her out of the water should have been her own. And yet, for the blink of an eye, it was old Lodger. "It's safe now," he seemed to be telling her. "It's safe now."

And so it was. Bryna and Ki-ya made the crossing easily. The broken stones from the storm-damaged bridge sat high above the waterline, and made a perfect causeway. They didn't even get their paws wet.

Up until that point Ki-ya had always been out in front urging them on. But now, all of a sudden, it was Bryna who was leading the way and Ki-ya who followed silently behind, his close presence her only reassurance. He did not question the ways she took, more confident in her ability than she was herself.

And would any dog even listen to her – let alone accept their crazy idea – rather than kill her on the spot? Kill them both!

The air, heavy with the scent of cats on the north side of the river began to change. Old dog scent. New dog scent. Fewer and fewer cats. All the time, fewer and fewer cats.

They stopped once, suddenly agitated, as the reek of the Booga began to hurt their noses. There were carcasses too, left to rot in the middle of the road; three small dogs together, their broken bodies heaped in a pile like bags of rubbish. But this was an old kill. Days old, probably.

The heavy bank of cloud above them broke open for a moment and the sun's warmth spilled down upon their backs. Bryna pushed on, striding confidently, up and away from the river. She knew, at last, where she was going and she did not need to think her way. Bryna was on her way home . . . to The Lonnen.

Soon only the smell of dogs reached their noses.

"Where are they?" Ki-ya asked. "I can smell them, but I can't see them."

"Here somewhere," said Bryna. "I'll bet my claws on it."

To Ki-ya the door they stopped in front of looked no different to any other door, in a street that looked no different to any other street. He watched as Bryna became strangely fidgety. She was not scared, this was something quite different. The downstairs window of the house had been broken out at some time. The broken glass was all but gone now, and the empty framework was criss-crossed, rutted and scored, where leaping paws had clawed their marks in passing. Many, many dogs had come and gone that way. Their stench was over-powering.

Bryna sat down in front of the window as if she was waiting for something. Ki-ya's fur bristled, his body and tail became puffed and bloated as the mixture of dog scents filled his head, turned his stomach. He sat himself at her side, as best he could.

The longer they sat there, the more ridiculous the whole adventure seemed to be. And if the cats sensed it, maybe the dogs did too. The streets began to close in around them. Fresh scents began to betray the presence of the dogs. There were eyes and ears too, noses, tongues and teeth, all taking them in, all seeing them in their own way. And there was no way out for a cat. No way back.

Then came the heavy pad-padding of paws and the scuffing of claws against the pavement. Not a pack though. One dog. Just one dog. Ki-ya began to turn his head.

"No, be still," Bryna said under her breath. "Wait a little longer."

The scratching of paws stopped close behind them, and a laboured dog's breath ruffled the fur at the back of their necks. For a very long time the dog stood silently behind them, studying them carefully. Bemused, astounded perhaps, curious, most certainly. It was the dog's curiosity that saved them then.

"Why, I ask myself?" the dog said, at last breaking his silence. "Why?" The cats decided this was not really a question for them and stayed quiet. They were right. "A three-legged vagabond and his she-cat. Why would they walk calmly into the heart of a dog pack? Tell me, why would they do that?"

"We must speak with you," began Bryna. "We must—"

"Must!" growled the dog. "Must speak with us! My brothers – do you hear this cat?" He was suddenly howling with laughter. At the end of the street, answering yelps and howls parodied his, like a distant echo. "Why?" He asked again, as if this was the best part of the joke. "Why *must* you speak with us?"

"Oh bother why!" Ki-ya spat, finally losing his patience. "Why, why, why—" He turned on the dog, his tail lifted, his fur bristling with hate.

The dog's laughter became an instant warning growl, and the echoes at the end of the street growled with him.

As dog and cat stanced, faced each other down, Bryna moved between them, and as she did she saw for the first time who this dog was.

"Kim? Kim. Don't you know me? Don't you know who I am? It's Bryna – see." She pushed her face into his, so close she could taste the wash of his sour breath. The old dog strained his eyes to see her more clearly. His nose, dry and white with age, sniffed at her.

"We *must* talk to you," she repeated.

Kim turned his head away from her. He was laughing again, but quietly now, deep in his throat. "You have some nerve, cat, you and your friend here . . ." He paused. Almost unnoticed, a group of dogs had gathered at Kim's side. Bryna recognised the terrier, Yip-yap, among them. More dogs were closing in. The smell of excitement was lifting their ears, lifting their tails; it shone coldly in their eyes. Desire was filling them up inside. The desire to hunt. The desire to kill.

Kim was an old dog, half-blind, his senses dull. And yet the pack did not attack. They held back behind him, as if waiting for a signal. "This was a foolishness, Bryna," he said. "There's a scar on my belly that tells me you saved my life once. But that debt is paid."

"Please . . . you must listen to what I have to say."

"Why do you waste your breath on them?"

cried Yip-yap, snarling at Bryna as he spoke. "I too know these cats. And I've got my own belly wound to remind me of their claws!"

The sound of yowls and growls grew louder. Ki-ya moved closer to Bryna. If they were going to die, they would die together, give as good as they got. Death would not be one-sided. There would be no running away this time, no flight.

Bryna's hackles should have lifted then. She should have bared her teeth, opened her claws. Attacked before they were attacked. But she did not. Fighting to the death would simply have given the Booga what it desired most. She had to make the dogs understand. She just had to.

Without thinking, she lay down, turned deliberately on to her back, belly up, defenceless. Like she was playing a silly game of begging-kitten with Mrs Ida Tupps.

Ki-ya stared at her in disbelief. And yet,

beyond all reason, he found himself copying her. He too lay down, turned belly up, shut his eyes, and waited for his death.

"Kill us then," cried Bryna. "We'll not fight back. We'll not struggle. Kill us. And let's see what that achieves!"

"Two fewer bloody cats for a start," Yip-yap laughed.

"And when other cats come after us to avenge our deaths?"

"Well, we'll bloody well kill them too!"

"Or they you," said Bryna.

"Aye well – that won't be any concern of yours, will it?" said Yip-yap.

"No, I suppose not . . . but tell me, who will protect your puppies from the Booga then?"

Yip-yap began to laugh again, but his laugh dissolved in his throat. A strange, puzzled silence had fallen over the dog pack.

"Go on then – take your vengeance out

on us. If that's all it takes to make you feel better?" Bryna goaded them. "We're making it easy for you . . . Or . . . or dare you turn your anger against your *real* enemy?"

Unsure growls and murmured threats grew up again.

"What are you saying, cat? Would you set us against Dread Booga, now?" Kim said, his body shaking with rage. But something in Bryna's words stopped him from attacking her.

"Do you think we're *that* stupid, cat?" snarled Yip-yap. "There isn't a dog who can run up against its power. Khan's death taught us that much. Let's finish this now!"

"No dog," Kim growled. "The foolish cat wanted to talk. Let her talk."

"There is not *one* dog," said Bryna. "Not one, not five together even—"

"Not twenty-five!" barked Yip-yap. "We've all seen this creature's work."

"No, not twenty-five dogs," Bryna agreed.

"Not twenty-five dogs, not twenty-five cats, either." She hesitated a moment. "Alone we are weak and small, but dogs and cats together . . ." There were more murmurs, growls and nervous laughs.

"But dogs *and* cats," repeated Bryna, "fighting together as one . . ."

"Together, *against* Dread Booga?" The idea was madness. As loony as the pair of daft cats who had walked into The Lonnen and presented themselves at Kim's feet for execution.

"Together," said Ki-ya.

"Together . . ." said Kim, thoughtfully. He was getting tired, had had enough excitement for one afternoon, and his insides were grumbling with wind again. "Well, cat . . . Bryna-not-so-foolish, go home. Spread your message, gather together your cats – if you can – and I will gather the dogs. When it's done we'll talk again. I will call you to a Council. Now, go home . . ."

Dart's Idea

And so, Bryna and Ki-ya did not die that day. When they stood up and calmly walked away from the dogs, who could tell who was the more amazed?

Twenty-one

THE GATHERING-IN

"There you are, Lugger. I told you so," said Treacle excitedly, to the small brown rag-a-tat of a cat who sat at his side. And then he shouted, "Ki-ya, Bryna, over here." He became so overexcited he fell off the stone he was balanced on and ducked himself in the river. A second brown cat, looking just as tatty as the first, but almost twice as big, calmly dipped his paw into the water and pulled him out again. Treacle didn't seem to notice that he'd been in the water. "Ki-ya—" he called again.

All afternoon, Treacle had been waiting patiently on the broken stonework of the bridge with his odd collection of cats. There were six of them, and they all looked and smelled very much the same. "They've been living in the sewers," he explained. "That's why they're this odd colour, and the funny smell—" he stopped himself with an embarrassed laugh. "Sorry Lugger, didn't mean to offend. Anyway, there's lots more where they came from."

"Lots more where we came from, Captain," echoed the small brown cat called Lugger, who hadn't taken offence at all.

Ki-ya sniffed the air disapprovingly, but said nothing.

"They've been living on rats. There's nothing but rats to eat down there. They're great rat catchers."

"Great rat catchers, Captain," said Lugger. All six cats nodded together.

"They didn't believe me at first; about the alliance with the dogs. Said you couldn't do it."

"Said you couldn't do it, Captain."

"Cats and dogs together, I told them."

"He told us, Captain."

"But you have done it, haven't you? I mean, they are going to help us, aren't they?"

"Well, er, well . . ." Bryna, hesitated. She looked at Ki-ya, and his eyes smiled back at her. "Yes," she said more definitely, "yes, they are going to help."

"Yes, they are going to help!" repeated Lugger, triumphantly, eyeing his companions as if he defied any cat among them to disagree. "Right then, Captain, call us when you're wanting us." He touched his nose with his paw. "You know where we are." Each of the six cats lifted a paw and pointed solemnly to the ground.

"Eh?" said Treacle. "Oh er, yes, yes of course."

With that the sewer cats collected themselves into a shambling single file, and with Lugger at the front marched themselves off down the riverbank towards an exposed sewer outfall. There was a heavy, broken iron grille leaning across the entrance. Exactly how they managed to move it is something of a mystery, but between them, and with a great deal of disorganised pulling and pushing, heaving and yanking, the iron grill inched aside. Then, one after another they disappeared into the dark hole.

"I hope we haven't lost them for good," said Bryna.

Ki-ya sniffed the air, smiled to himself, and said nothing.

It was well into the next day before Dart reappeared in the wood. She came in the company of two cats: both big, heavily built toms, fighters no doubt, but house-cats for all that. One was a short-haired, creamy-white moggie and the other a grey tabby. Shelley and Tibs she called them; from a small lodge in Waverley Crescent. They'd both left their mates and kits behind, but had followed Dart more out of a sense of boredom than for any real belief in her idea.

When Dart had settled them with something to eat she went to talk with the others.

"It's no good," she said. "I've been on the streets all night. Of the few cats I could coax out of their hidey-holes, most of them think we're completely mad. Only two cats, two out of the lot of them, would come with me."

"I . . . I brought six," offered Treacle, self-consciously.

"Sewer cats!" said Ki-ya, twisting his nose against their scent as if it still lingered on the air. "What would they know about fighting a Booga?"

"What do any of us, come to that!" said Bryna. "We'll just have to keep trying. We must make cats listen. What else can we do?"

"If Kim has as much trouble convincing the dogs—"

"We'll fight with whatever strength we

can muster." Bryna's tail flicked with agitation.

"And if we end up dead, it will all be the same anyway," said Dart.

Somewhere out across the town a streak of lightning flashed through the sky, and the sound of thunder roared, broke their argument, settled it for good.

Ki-ya, Dart, Treacle and Bryna took to travelling openly about the town, talking to any cat they happened upon. Often they went in the company of dogs sent by Kim to add weight to their message. (That they didn't fall victim to the prowling Booga was no miracle; only their luck and another's misfortune). Those cats who listened to them passed the message on in turn. Sometimes given seriously and worried over, sometimes whispered like so much tittle-tattle, often joked about. The story of the crazy cats and dogs who had made an alliance, and together were going to kill Dread Booga. To some, the message was a disease, the talk of which was cut short with the cuff of a paw, or worse, met with deaf ears. Yet for a few, and at first the few were a very few, there was an answer in this dangerous idea. Slowly cats began to collect around the deserted farmhouse at the fringes of the wood. Others boldly called out across the town, sending messages of support in the deep silences of the night. They would come, give them the day and the hour, they would come.

And then, where there had been chatter, argument, secret discussions and tacit agreements, suddenly the streets of the town fell silent and still. Visiting stopped. There were no more new arrivals at the wood. Prowls for food ranged closer and closer to lodges. And there were no squeals of kits at play, no midnight romances, no jealous territorial fights.

The gathering-in was done.

Twenty-two

THE GREAT COUNCIL

On a warm, cloudless afternoon Bryna and Ki-ya sat together on the riverbank, watching the gentle waters slowly trickling past. They had prowled there more for something to do than for any real need; beyond Bryna's simple desire to sit quietly with Ki-ya as she had taken to doing.

Bryna dangled a paw carelessly into the rippling waters. She was thinking about old Lodger, about Dexter and strange Fat Blossom, about Mrs Ida Tupps and days gone by. She tried to force a smile into her eyes. Ki-ya pressed his flanks closer to hers for comfort, and tried to smile with her.

The sun began to drop in the evening

sky, turning the colour of the river from a dazzling silver to a rusty orange. The broken stones of the bridge stood up black and disfiguring, like the cracked teeth of some ancient cat, yet solid and immoveable above the shimmering waters.

But then the stones did move. Or at least, something moved across them creating that illusion. An animal, smaller than a man, larger than a cat.

Bryna and Ki-ya sat up, stared with concentration, their noses searching for a scent. It was Yip-yap.

The terrier walked purposefully towards them, his tail and head held high and proud. Without looking at them he sat down at their side.

"Tomorrow," he said. And that was all he said. It was such a simple message, and yet not one to be entrusted to another. It was the call to the Great Council, and yet there was so much more in that word. Tomorrow.

Tomorrow was life or death. Tomorrow was success or failure. And either way, tomorrow was a world changed forever.

The three allies sat on in silence. The sun disappeared behind the outlines of the buildings that made up their horizon. The edge of their town. The very edge of their world, their lives even. And beyond? . . . Beyond, like tomorrow, was another unknown.

Yip-yap crept away as the growing darkness turned into a final starlit black.

The Great Council was held out in the open, on the Town Moor. Five cats, five dogs sitting together in a circle. And if Dread Booga decided to join their circle? Well, no place was safe now.

"And how *exactly* do you suggest this killing is made, cat?" Kim asked. "After all, this adventure is of your making." Bryna sat looking vacantly at Ki-ya. Beside her, Treacle fidgeted nervously. How was this killing to be made? Planning and campaign was not the way of the cat. Nor, for that matter, was it the way of the dog. There was instinct, there was survival, there was tooth and claw, and there was the hunt that filled their bellies. There was nothing else.

Or . . . or was there?

Bryna's head began to ache, filling up with that dullness of thought that made the real cats and dogs around her seem like nothing more than faint shadows. And yet, inexplicably, at the same time her senses seemed to sharpen. For one brief moment she was certain Dexter and Beacon had joined their circle. "The town must have eyes," Beacon seemed to be saying. "The town must have ears."

"Eyes and ears," Bryna repeated vaguely, and the ghosts were gone.

"What's that, cat?" Yip-yap snapped.

"Eh? Oh – we, we must give the town eyes . . . I mean, I mean . . ." And then she was suddenly sure of herself. She remembered Dexter's Intelligence and Beacon's beautiful, ever-watchful eyes. She stood up boldly and faced the gathering. "I mean, we must set watchers across the town, keen watchers to look out for the Booga. Whenever it appears, whenever there is sight or sound of it we must know at once. And then we must act upon it. Together, swiftly, decisively."

"Yes, oh yes, Bryna," said Ki-ya, excitedly. "Our weight of numbers must see that it's done."

"Hah! Brave words, cat," said Kim. "But it's a big town. Where are all these dogs and cats you speak of? It would take more than our entire number just to keep a guard at each street corner." Yip-yap began to snitter.

"And even if the Booga was found this way, how can a call be sent quickly enough to bring us all running together? Or perhaps you can give the town a voice to go with its eyes and its ears?"

Suddenly dogs *and* cats were laughing. Bryna looked at Ki-ya, uncertain now. Too many questions, too few answers! It was then that Treacle found the courage to call out. "I think there is a way!" he said. "Through the sewers."

"Through the sewers, Captain," echoed Lugger, who'd been invited by Bryna (on Treacle's insistence) to join the Great Council.

"What?" asked Yip-yap.

"Under the town – through the sewers. Wherever there's a street there's a sewer. It's a–a sort of a big tunnel running underneath it."

"Tunnel running underneath, Captain."

Kim wasn't laughing now. He remembered long ago, as a pup, watching rainwater running through the gutters, remembered it disappearing down through the iron grilles in the roads and wondering where it could all be going. But then he shook his head.

"Yes, cat, but even you aren't small enough to pass that way."

Treacle stood up triumphantly. "No, no I'm not. But my voice is. My voice *is!* That's how I discovered Lugger in the first place. I heard him whispering from deep down in the sewers. His voice came right up at me through the drains. Nearly scared the life out of me."

"Scared the life out of him, Captain."

"Treacle, you're a genius!" cried Bryna. "What quicker way is there of raising the alarm? *And* we've already got the cats to do the job."

Commander in charge of communications, that's what Ki-ya nicknamed Treacle then. "M–Me!" He stuttered with absolute delight. And it was agreed by the Great Council, it would be Treacle's job – with Lugger's help of course – to raise the alarm.

Kim wasn't finished. "This is all very well and good; watchers and waiters, listeners and callers spread all over the town. But even using the sewers I still say our numbers would be spread too thinly to make a decisive attack. We must act as one body, a body large enough to bring down Dread Booga. It's our only chance."

The excitement began to fade from Treacle's face. Bryna felt lost, and suddenly out of her depth. "What are you suggesting?"

"A trap," said Kim, quietly. "A trap set wide enough to lure Dread Booga out into the open . . . tight enough to keep *us* together. The riverside streets would be best. The alarm could be raised easily from there. And there are plenty of dark alleyways for animals to hide in. Plenty of dead-ends to make escape impossible."

"Yes, but what *kind* of a trap?" asked Bryna, her tail gently licking the ground with worry.

Kim looked at Yip-yap.

"Boom, boom," said the terrier, slowly and

thoughtfully. "Boom, boom, boom. Let the Booga give itself away with the sound of its own thunder."

"Oh, yes," Dart hissed. "What are you going to do, Kim? Ask some poor sucker of a cat to stand in the middle of the road and cry 'Come and get me Booga'; to go and get themselves killed! That would be right. That would be the dogs' way!" As she spat Kim began to growl threateningly.

"Stop this." Ki-ya sprang to his feet. "Stop this!"

They froze. Angry. Shocked. And yet . . . and yet, when it came down to it, what other way was there? Some animal – cat or dog – would have to do just that. Set itself up as a target. Get itself killed—

"I will do it," said Bryna, softly, getting to her feet.

"Me too," said Yip-yap. He stood up at her side. "We will need others; as many as will do it. Volunteers. No animal can be ordered to its own death . . ." There he ran out of words, and the meeting fell into a deep brooding silence.

Shadows fell across the town with the coming of night. The Great Council was done. Dogs and cats slunk warily away.

Twenty-three

LIVE BAIT

Before the sun rose again cats and dogs were moving secretly about the town. Watchers were set to watch; dogs and cats by strict timetable. And Treacle had been dispatched with Lugger and his sewer cats down into their dirty tunnels.

Bryna stood alone on the street. Out in the open, exposed and nervous. Live bait to hook Dread Booga. There was a cold wind in the air that stung her nose. It mixed up old and new scents, threw them at her, carried them away again. Above the rooftops of the town it hurled the clouds about in the same couldn't-care-less manner. It would rain soon. She looked about her. What street was this? Beggars Lane, Kim had called it. There were houses and gardens; gates pushed open by the wind clanged shut again. Cars stood idle at the side of road, their bodies rocking gently in the wind.

Inside her head the shadows of ghosts were moving again, and somehow they seemed more real than all of this. The town streets were the illusion, the dream. This was such a very ordinary day. Such an ordinary street.

For a moment she thought she caught a voice on the wind. Remembered the other dogs and cats standing on other streets, waiting like her to be victims. And she remembered the other paws somewhere down below her, at that very moment scampering through the sewers, their owners eager to catch any sound that might reach them from the outside world. Perhaps from the safety of some nearby doorway, or high rooftop, other eyes were watching her now? Would it be her death throes they would witness; a thunder-clap that was her end that would reveal their quarry, seal the Booga's fate as it sealed hers? She shuddered, pretending it was the wind, and backed away from her invisible enemy. She wanted to close her eyes, wanted desperately to hide away, but knew she must not. There was a big red car at the roadside behind her. She crouched down low in front of it, as if the weight of its presence could give her some protection.

When would the creature come? Get it over with. Finish it. She almost wished it was there now. But Dread Booga did not come. Not yet . . .

Yip-yap sniffed at the nearest lamppost, like he always did, cocked his leg, like he always did. Stood his ground in the open. From Tullyhole Street the ground dropped steeply downhill. He could see the corner of Spittle Rows, and further to Monk Street, Beggars Lane and the riverside. And, if he looked carefully, here and there he could see another cat, another dog waiting anxiously, just as he was. He lifted his nose to the air and let his lungs fill up with the cold, early morning air. It told him nothing. Nothing yet . . .

Treacle sat in his sewer beneath the ground and worried. Not worried over anything in particular, just worried. Everything was set. Every fifty or sixty paces one of Lugger's cats sat listening. Maybe at a junction – a crossroads – of drainage pipes, maybe at the opening of an outlet pipe, maybe directly below a manhole, where the thin slits in the iron cover let them see all the way to the sky, and more importantly let them hear and smell the streets above them. It had come as a revelation to Treacle just how easily, and how far, sound travelled through the sewers. He'd tested the system endlessly since returning from the Great Council. Lugger must have been more than a prowl's length away when he'd called him back the last time; and it had been nothing more than a whisper. In fact, it had almost worked too well. The slight noises he'd made had passed out on to the streets at several points and almost caused a panic among the dogs and cats who heard them.

After that Treacle had ordered an immediate silence in the sewers. No more messages were to be called out loud. No tom fooling, no kittish games, no sniggering, and positively, absolutely positively, no purring. (Not that there was a cat among them who had the heart to purr that morning.) There was to be only one more call: the raising of the alarm.

Treacle knew almost to a cat and dog where every animal was; or at least knew where Bryna and Kim had planned them to be. Knew the bolt holes. Knew the hidden doorways where groups of animals lurked, eagerly awaiting the call to attack. Knew the garden hedge behind which proud Ki-ya stood with Shelley and Tibs. He knew the darkened alleyway where Kim was waiting patiently with his pack. He even knew the rooftop perches where nameless cats sat, the riverside haunts where unknown dogs lay panting among long grass.

He knew about the runners, with Dart at their head, posted at the exit of the great sewer outflow on the riverside. Knew they were listening for the call. And knew that when it came they would quickly begin the charge to bring down Dread Booga.

Every now and again paws would pat-a-pat lightly through the sewers. Cats passing information on to cats, each sentry walking only as far as the next and then back to its own watch. And so news travelled down the line, until it arrived at Treacle.

Treacle, it seemed, knew everything. So, he sat, and he worried, and he waited for the call.

But there was no call. Not yet . . .

Kim pulled with his teeth at the tats of hair

in his old greying coat. He grumbled about his poor stomach, relieved himself with a fart and felt much better for it . . . Ki-ya licked clean the already clean fur of his short front leg . . . Treacle scratched his ear and worried . . . And Bryna?

Bryna sat—

No, Bryna stood up, suddenly anxious, at the sound of heavy footfall. She listened. Two feet . . . two feet moving towards her, unworried at the noise they made . . . But not *that* close. Not in her street. How far away? How far?

Crack! Crack! Crack!

A brilliant slither of white light burst across the sky with each explosion, faded instantly away and was gone. Behind it an echo bounced angrily off the walls of the buildings and rumbled away down through the streets towards the river. *Murder, murder*, it seemed to roar!

Dread Booga moved slowly towards the

body of its victim, an odd gurgling sound – almost a sigh of relief – escaping from the side of its mouth as it took each deliberate step.

Crack! Crack! Crack!

Dead already. Not dead enough.

Close by a dog looked on. Stunned, frozen with fear, he could not move. Could not make his call. He had seen the killing made. Was watching the Booga still as it moved clumsily down the street towards him. But where was his bark to make his call? Far below the ground echoes of thunder were still grumbling through the drains. The noise filled the dog's head, ran shivering through his poor useless frozen body, killing the cat over and over again.

"Here!" He yowled at last, forcing the words from his stricken lungs. "Bloody well here! The Booga's bloody well here! In Monk Street. MONK STREET! You get that? You get that, you crazy cats—?"

Crack! Crack! Crack!

And then, suddenly, there was running. Perhaps paws started moving even before the dog died, before the first catcalls from the sewers, the crack of thunder stunning them into action. And if at first it was senseless stumblings, blind panic without direction or thought, when Treacle cried out "Monk Street", it became a charge.

First it was the runners, lead by Dart. Calling the others out, pulling them out of their hiding-places even, with nips and bites or cries of encouragement. Dogs and cats piled into the empty streets. From doorways and rooftop perches. From the branches of trees and the insides of dustbins. From the hilltop and from the riverside. Out they poured, more and more again. And they headed in one direction.

The Booga stood over the body of the dog, its second victim of the day, and it was puzzled. It had been a strange animal;

just standing there barking its head off. Yowling into the gutters. Almost asking to be killed, mad beggar. Well, Dread Booga had obliged.

At the bottom of Monk Street a dog and a cat suddenly ran out into the middle of the road. Of these two animals no names are known to remember them by. They were simply a dog and a cat. A dog and a cat running together, side by side, charging the Booga down.

They did not get within thirty strides of Dread Booga before its thunder brought them to the ground. Stilled their run forever. Left them lying side by side in death, as their last moments had been spent in life. But as they fell, more animals turned into the street. Seven – eight – nine, together. Then more, and more still. Running hard, forgetting all fear. Willing themselves on as they answered the call.

The Booga snarled, as inside its injured

head it felt the first tug of fear. "Troo farr ap eeeee—" It squealed out loud. And the foulness of that squeal was almost enough to stop them in their stride. Almost, but not quite. This time it would take the thunder to do that.

More and more animals then.

Ki-ya appeared with Shelley and Tibs, making their attack from a side street. Then came Yip-yap among a pack of dogs ten strong. Behind them, and closing fast, were an even larger, mixed group of animals who had joined in with Dart's mad run from the riverside.

Still the Booga squealed. "Raith kun, I sa!" Thunder roared, and no dog or cat came within striking distance before they fell.

"Don't bunch up!" yelled Ki-ya. "Spread out. Spread yourselves out! Don't make yourselves such easy targets."

And when, somewhere among the attack,

Kim heard Ki-ya's cries he howled in his turn, "On, dogs! On, cats! Harder! Faster!"

Another dog, another cat fell dead.

As Ki-ya approached the Booga from the side, Kim came at him from the front.

Then Shelley stumbled, his life flowing out of him. No pain. Just time for one clear thought of his mate and their kits, and then the final darkness.

Ki-ya was very close now. His ears ran with blood, hearing dulled to a rumble by the roaring of the thunder. But his teeth weren't dulled. At last he was close enough to strike. The Booga plucked a streak of fire right out of the sky, and hurled it. The death of a dog at Ki-ya's side gave him his chance. He leapt. His anger, his frustration, his pain, all went into that leap. As he flew he sensed the Booga's fear; smelled it like a foul scent clinging to its flimsy body. Smelled something else too . . . its madness.

The blows Ki-ya landed were not decisive.

The creature was already turning to find its next victim as he made contact. Ki-ya snapped his teeth closed around what he hoped was an ear, and at the same time, felt the claws of his good front paw rake the leathery skin of its face. Then he felt himself thrown roughly aside. Tossed, with a strange curse, to the ground. Again thunder began its evil roar, its reek filled the air.

Kim lunged forward then, but not at the Booga's face, at its supporting leg. He gained a hold and bit deep, only to be kicked violently. Kicked again, until he was forced to let go. Then Yip-yap was there, playing copy-cat. He clamped his jaws tightly around the same leg, tearing the skin to the bone. Held on. Wouldn't let go.

The crack crackle of lightning, the deep rolling growls of thunder barely covered the sound of the Booga's agonising squeals, or Yip-yap's final yowl . . .

*　　*　　*

Bryna had heard the very first roar of thunder. Smelled its foul stench. Had stood stricken and confused, unable to move until a voice startled her into action. "Come on, cat, didn't you hear Treacle's call? You can't skulk about here, while Bryna herself's getting killed for you!"

"But I'm, but I'm—"

A cat ran past her. It had white paws; she remembered that much because, as it ran, she ran after it and its white paws kicked up and down in her face.

With almost every step more animals joined them. First cats, and then dogs too. Together they were swept eagerly along.

The sounds of thunder began to come more quickly to them. More direct. No longer echoed through drains or bounced off the walls of buildings. Beckoning them on almost, daring them to come closer.

And suddenly, there was Dread Booga. Dread Booga moving awkwardly towards them. Not them towards it. Its surprise not theirs. Thunder roared again and White-paws fell in front of her. It all happened too quickly. No time to think.

The animals around Bryna seemed to be dissolving away as the thunder roared and roared, as the sky lit up with fire and lashed down upon them. The more animals there were the more powerfully the Booga struck out. Some – a lot – fell instantly dead, some crawled away to die alone. Others simply fled, scared for their lives.

And then she saw that the Booga was limping. Limping badly. Its leg bloodied and torn. And as it lumbered forward it dragged something along the ground with it, like a dirty rag. Like . . . a dog.

"Yip-yap?" Even in death his jaws were still closed tightly around the Booga's leg.

A streak of light tore open the sky again.

Bryna stopped running. Close by there was an alleyway. A certain dead-end. She began to slink slowly backwards into its darkness. She did not move out of fear, was not running away. She retreated quite deliberately. And in the darkness she stood still. Waited. The Booga was getting near, bringing itself to her.

But how could she finish it? How could she possibly bring down Dread Booga? She suddenly felt so small, so very small and useless. And the creature seemed so huge, so powerful and dangerous.

Her head began to ache. Shadows were falling, clouding her mind. Filling her head with images of the dead, faces she did not want to see.

"Oh no, not now. Please, not now. You're all dead," she cried out in desperation. "All dead and ghosts! And I need help. *Real* help."

But there was only the dead.

Grundle was the very first at her side, snarling and spitting; the tiny bird on his back frantically beating its wings, cack-cackering noisily. Behind him came Beacon. And then Dexter, beautiful Dexter, and Fat Blossom . . .

"Lodger – is–is that really you?" And it *was* Lodger.

The Booga came on. Almost there now. Almost there. It raised its clawed fingers.

Bryna's gasp of surprise was met by another noise. A raw squeal, and not made by any animal in pain.

Suddenly there was a new fear about the creature. Something Bryna had never smelled before.

"But . . . Then you can see them, too?" said Bryna. "You can see the ghosts—" The Booga's eyes stood wide open, glaring white in its terror, staring right through her to something else. Bryna followed its gaze. Behind Beacon surely there was Maxwell, Crumpet with her kits, Brindle and a pair of black toms. And behind Lodger there was White-paws, and Yip-yap and great Khan. More and more were joining them all the time. The dead. The dead, killed by the Booga that very day.

Suddenly Bryna's ghosts were moving forward. Beginning to attack, together—

Thunder roared again. Just once. That was all the time Dread Booga had left to it. No victim fell. But there was a searing flash of light, a blinding light. Bryna tried to see through it, but she could not. Its brilliance filled her eyes, filled her head too, and did not fade away. And with the light there was pain. Her pain. But not her pain, somehow. Distant and detached.

Around her there were the noises of a fight. A desperate, desperate struggle. The horrid death struggle of some poor demented creature, as it thrashed mindlessly about, as it tried in vain to save itself. Thankfully, the light inside Bryna's head began to fade, turning first to thin pricks of icy grey and then to deepest, silent black.

Bryna knew no more . . .

Twenty-four

ENDINGS AND BEGINNINGS

Bryna never opened her eyes again. Was she dead? No, not dead. Although at first she was sure she must be. There was no pain, only a strange sickening numbness, and it was dark. At least, it was dark on the outside of her head, where her eyes should have been showing her the world. And inside her head? Well, inside her head it wasn't dark at all. That surprised her; just how light it really was inside her head, when outside it was so very dark.

And her ghosts were still there, sitting quietly around her. That was another surprise; it seems you don't really need eyes to see ghosts.

Bryna stretched out her legs, cautiously tested them on the ground before fumbling her way to her feet. She tried to feel her way forwards, to take a few steps, but blind she could not tell where she was walking; whichever way she turned her path seemed to be blocked by the bodies of the dead.

As her senses sharpened she took a deep breath. There were still real smells to smell; not coming from the inside of her head, but from the streets. The mixed-up scent of dogs and cats . . . the sweet smell of their freshly spilled blood. She lifted her ears, tried to follow the flight of a bird as it gave its panic cry far above her. Then she heard the gentle sounds of the river and she turned her head that way.

Wherever she stumbled her ghosts followed after her. But they did not try to guide her, their work was done. To survive she had to learn the ways of her new, dark world on her own . . .

*　　*　　*

Ki-ya, Kim, Dart and Treacle found Bryna between them; at the bottom of some over-grown back garden, sniffing blindly for food at a long-dried-out old dustbin. They had searched endlessly for her most of that day, most of that night too; had almost given up hope.

Earlier they had come across the body of the creature . . . Dread Booga. Curled up in death it looked so fragile, so timid even. And small; hardly bigger than a large dog. They could not make out what had brought about its death. One of its thin legs was cut to the bone where Yip-yap had planted his teeth, and the gnarled skin on the side of its pale grey face was slashed where Ki-ya had clawed his mark. But where was the death wound? Apart from the old scar on its head there were no other wounds at all. Nothing that might have killed it.

But they knew little of the ways of ghosts or creatures of spirit, and now, with Bryna found, they did not want to think too much about the Booga's death. Dread Booga was dead, Bryna was alive, and that was enough for them.

Silently – for somehow this was not the time for words – they led her out of that garden, and began to work their way slowly down through the dark empty streets, towards the riverside. They walked together, dog and cats side by side as equals. And they walked upon the roads, out in the open. Unhurried. Unthreatened. Free.

The pale golden cracks of dawn began to show through the weight of solid black cloud. All across the town it touched the very tips of the rooftops, caught upon the leaves of the trees, sprinkled its light upon the river. Lifting their hearts, heralding the beginning of a new day . . .

SPILLING THE MAGIC

Stephen Moore

Staying with boring relatives, life looks bleak for Billy and Mary until they find . . .

A strange book of spells.

Whisked into the mysterious, multi-coloured world of Murn they find a world on its last legs.

A world knee-deep in spilt magic.

Even with the help of flying pigs and a vegetarian dragon, can they put the magic back where it belongs?

h HODDER

Another Hodder Children's book

OWL LIGHT
A W. H. Smith Mind Boggling book

Maggie Pearson

'I'm going to be a werewolf!' said Ellie.

Under the owl light everything changes shape. Ellie disappears at night-time. Could she really be the werewolf Hal dreads in his imagination?

The common is a wild, forbidden place, a place of mysterious sounds, home to threatened badgers and the haunt of intriguing neighbours . . .

ORDER FORM